Once A Hero

The Story of Private Wojtek Bear
WWII SOLDIER

James A. Cutchin

outskirtspress
DENVER, COLORADO

This is a work of fiction. The events and characters described herein are imaginary and are not intended to refer to specific places or living persons. The opinions expressed in this manuscript are solely the opinions of the author and do not represent the opinions or thoughts of the publisher. The author has represented and warranted full ownership and/or legal right to publish all the materials in this book.

Once A Hero
The Story of Private Wojtek Bear WWII Soldier
All Rights Reserved.
Copyright © 2015 James A. Cutchin
v2.0

Cover Illustrated by: James A. Cutchin.
Cover © 2015 James A. Cutchin and thinkstockphotos.com. All rights reserved - used with permission.

This book may not be reproduced, transmitted, or stored in whole or in part by any means, including graphic, electronic, or mechanical without the express written consent of the publisher except in the case of brief quotations embodied in critical articles and reviews.

Outskirts Press, Inc.
http://www.outskirtspress.com

Paperback ISBN: 978-1-4787-6288-1
Hardback ISBN: 978-1-4787-6289-8

Outskirts Press and the "OP" logo are trademarks belonging to Outskirts Press, Inc.

PRINTED IN THE UNITED STATES OF AMERICA

I dedicate this book to my children:

Alisa

Jamie

California

Bart

Alexis

Acknowledgments

I would like to thank the following people for their suggestions, advice or encouragement: Margaret Waldroff, Marcia L. Cutchin, and Paula Keyser.

CHAPTER I

This Is a Story of a Bear. He Was Not Just Any Ole Bear. This Bear Helped to Win a War.

Our story begins in the forest of Iran. A baby cub was born to a Syrian brown mama bear. Mama Bear's baby was very small; he weighed only about one pound and was about six inches long. When bear cubs are born, they have no teeth, no hair and are blind. Without the care of their mothers, they would not survive. Mama Bear was so happy to have her baby. She said, "My baby must have a name. I will name him Cubby."

Every day Mama Bear would nurse Cubby while she lay on her side, and Cubby lay on her stomach. When Cubby was nursing, he would make a motor-like hum that let Mama Bear know everything was just as it should be. Mama Bear's milk was very nutritious, and Cubby grew a little every day. Before long his eyes opened, and he was able to see all the wonderful sights of the forest.

Bears move around a lot. They are constantly looking for food. A full-grown bear will eat forty-five pounds of food a day. Compare that to an adult human who eats about four pounds per day. When Cubby's mother would move from place to place, she would carry him in her mouth. Cubby loved the ride. Bears see in color, so he could see all the beautiful colors of the forest. A bear's eyesight is about the same as a human's vision. However, a bear's hearing and sense of smell are about 100 times greater than a human's senses. Before long Cubby could tell what lay ahead just by the way the forest smelled and the sounds he heard.

Mama Bear was very devoted to her little cub. She was very affectionate but strict and protective. Her primary concern was for his safety and education. Bears are very social creatures and learn by watching. Cubby carefully watched his mother in every move she made. He watched how she found food. He watched how she caught fish, how she climbed trees to get bee hives that contained honey and how she got very angry and chased off any predator that could harm her baby. Mama Bear did not have to worry about many predators. She was very strong and weighed about 30 stone or 420 pounds. She had huge teeth and six-inch claws on each of her paws. Although she was very big, she could run thirty miles an hour. That is as fast as the speed of a race horse. Mama Bear could swim, climb trees and walk right up the side of a mountain with the greatest of ease. Bears are also very intelligent. When you combine their physical abilities with their high intelligence, they become a very formidable foe indeed. Any creature who tried to come between Mama Bear and her cub was certain of a very drastic fate.

In the forest of Iran lurks a very crafty and deadly predator, the tiger. Tigers weigh about 29 stone or 400 pounds and are equipped with large, sharp teeth and six-inch retractable claws on each paw. A tiger can run thirty miles an hour, climb trees and swim across a five mile wide river. Tigers are a carnivore which means they only eat meat. When a tiger is hungry, any meat will do, even little bear cubs. Mama Bear could not always see the tiger because with his stripes and earth-tone colors, he could easily blend into the forest. He could hide in the tall grass or in a tree or maybe behind a fallen tree. Even though Mama Bear could not always see the tiger, the cat could not escape her keen sense of smell or excellent hearing. The tiger was a fierce predator, but he was no match for Mama Bear when she was protecting her cub.

As time moved forward, Cubby grew to about the size of a teddy bear. He played alongside his mother, running in and out between her legs, as she roamed through the forest searching for food. Bears like to eat all kinds of things. They are omnivores which mean they eat vegetables, fruit, berries, nuts and meat. The forest was so much fun for Cubby. He would chase birds, roll in the grass, and try to do everything he saw his mother do. He loved to wrestle. Anytime his mother took a break from searching for food, he would make her wrestle with him. He was always curious and eager to try new things.

One day he thought to himself that it was time to climb a tree. After all, he had seen his mother do it, and it looked easy. He spotted a tree he thought would be a good tree to climb, and he ran over and climbed about five feet up and stopped. Suddenly things looked different from up here. This was pretty high for a little bear cub. Cubby had a problem; he did not know how to get back down the tree. If he tried to turn around, he was sure he would fall. Cubby began to whimper. He was too afraid to go any further up the tree and did not know how to get back down. Mama Bear heard Cubby's weeping and headed to the rescue. When she reached the tree, she stood on her hind legs, gently grabbed Cubby by the back of the neck with her powerful jaws, and lowered him to the ground. Cubby stood there for a moment and immediately darted off to chase a butterfly as if nothing had ever happened. Every day was carefree and full of adventure for Cubby. His mother's vigilant eye was always on the lookout for anything that could harm her cub. Danger never entered Cubby's mind. He just wanted to know, "Is it time to eat?"

Suddenly a branch snapped. The snap was too loud to be made by any of the forest animals that Mama Bear knew. The animals in Mama Bear's forest walked softly. When a branch was snapped, even by the largest animals, the sound was a soft ping. Mama Bear's ears shot up. Her ears were pointed and alert. Something was not right. The forest was too quiet and still. The birds had stopped singing. A soft breeze began to blow through the trees. The breeze was filled with a smell unlike any smell Mama Bear had known before. There was danger in the air. Mama Bear began looking for Cubby. "Oh, where is my baby?"

she thought to herself as the smell of danger became stronger. Finally she saw him. After chasing the butterfly, he had ended up near a dense growth of bushes much farther from Mama Bear than he would have normally strayed. Mama Bear began to roar, "Run, Cubby, run!" Mama Bear began running with Cubby trying his best to keep up. He was running as fast as his little legs would carry him. Mama Bear kept urging him, "Hurry, Cubby, hurry!" A very loud boom rang out all across the forest. That boom changed Cubby's life forever. His mother, who was only a few feet in front of him, fell to her side. What had happened? Cubby did not understand. He ran up to his mother and got close to her face. Cubby rubbed his mother's nose with his nose. She did not move, and her nose was cold. Cubby was frightened and began to cry. Another boom rang out, and Cubby began to run. Cubby ran and ran. He did not stop until exhaustion overtook him, and the night had set in. Cubby's mother was dead. She had been killed by the deadliest creature on earth, the hunter.

We must now leave Cubby for a short while because our story takes us to another part of the world where a war was brewing. It was part of Cubby's destiny to help win that war. You may wonder how a bear could help win a war. Cubby, my dear readers, was not just any ole bear, as you shall see.

Our story continues in the country of Germany, where at this time, the German people are preparing for their biggest festival of the year.

CHAPTER II
Oktoberfest in Munich

In Bavaria, the Catholic region of Southern Germany, a young boy raced through the open pasture following an eagle overhead. The eagle knew that air did not rise over a forest or river. He soared high over fields and hills where the updrafts lifted his wings. To the east was the Danube River and to the south the snow-capped mountains of the Alps. What an incredible view the eagle had of this beautiful country!

The young man was named Hans. He wore thick knit Bavarian knee socks, knickers and a white shirt. Knickers are loose-fitting, short trousers that are gathered at the knees. Hans was a true Bavarian with dark brown eyes, brown hair and stocky build.

Bavaria is a place where people love their beer and have many festivals every year. From an eagle's viewpoint, the cities of Bavaria looked like a page from a fairy tale. All the houses had red roofs, and the doors and window shutters were painted in a rainbow of colors.

Hans knew he had to return home soon. But as he ran through the fields, he dreamed of what it would be like to fly like an eagle, high above the trees, watching the Danube River curve its way through the countryside. The eagle soared effortlessly with the speed of the wind. Oh, how Hans longed to fly! Reluctantly, Hans stopped at the top of the hill and turned to head home.

Hans found his mother standing at their chalet door, arms crossed, tapping her foot in mock (she was just pretending) anger waiting his return. A chalet is a wooden cottage with a gently sloping roof. The name chalet is Swiss and means small house. "Hurry, Hans, and get dressed in your festival clothes. Oktoberfest starts today," his mother said. Everyone was eager to get to the festival. Oktoberfest is a sixteen-day festival which begins late September and ends the first weekend of October.

The tradition of Oktoberfest began when a Bavarian prince and princess married in 1810. They gave a huge party and invited the entire town of Munich to attend. Munich was the capital city of Bavaria. The party was so popular, a tradition was started. Since then, at the same time each year, the people of Munich host the country's largest festival. The people of Germany have been enjoying Oktoberfest for over one hundred years.

The whole family would be dressed in their most festive outfits. Hans, his father and younger brother would be dressed in lederhosen (German for leather breeches), white shirts and suspenders to hold up their lederhosen. Hans' mother used her excellent embroidery skills to sew colorful designs on their lederhosen and suspenders. Embroidery is the craft of using needle and thread to stitch decorative pictures on materials such as fabric and leather. A Bavarian would know which city another Bavarian lived in just by the embroidery designs on his lederhosen. They would also each have a Bavarian hat called a tirolerhute. Hans had a green hat, his younger brother had a red hat and his father had a gray one. Hans' mother sewed a tuft (cluster) of goat hair on each hat. In Germany, goat hair is highly valued and prized. The more tufts of goat hair on your hat, the wealthier you are considered to be.

Hans' mother and sister would wear their best dirndls. A dirndl is a dress worn by women and young girls in Germany. A dirndl has many colorful embroidery designs sewn on the skirt and apron. The apron is considered a part of the dirndl. Hans knew his mother and father were very proud of their family and would want everyone to look their very best at the festival.

Oktoberfest was so much fun. There was music, lots of German sausage and splendidly decorated horse teams that pulled the giant wagons loaded with kegs of beer. The crowds dressed in colorful costumes were dancing to music played by the Om-pa-pa bands. Om-pa-pa bands are called that because of the sound the tubas make while keeping the beat or rhythm while other instruments play the melody. There were tree-climbing contests, strong man contests, and even contests to see which town had the best cheese. Young boys were allowed to drink beer, provided they did not drink too much and turn into a bierleichen (German for beer corpse). Hans and his younger brother Erich were allowed to freely roam the Oktoberfest from one end of town to the other. Erich was always called Bubi which means small boy in German. Erich's mother was the first to call him Bubi when he was just a baby. Soon Hans and his father were calling him Bubi. As Erich grew older, everyone knew him as Bubi. There were some in his hometown that did not know Erich was his real name.

While Hans and Bubi were enjoying the tree climbing contest, their mother and sister were strolling down Munich's stone paved roads admiring the embroidery designs and colors of the men's and boys' lederhosen and the women's and girls' dirndls. They were having a contest of their own, trying to be the first to guess where the people lived by the designs on their costumes. Hans' mother was named Eva and his sister's name was Hiya. Hiya was at the age where she shared her mother's work and, come Oktoberfest, she also shared her mother's excitement and joy of the festival.

Hans' father and his good friend, Father Josef, were watching the strong man contest. Hans' father's name was Werner. He and Father Josef had served together as infantry officers in the German Army in the First World War. Infantry soldiers are trained to fight on foot and sometimes engage the enemy in face-to-face combat. Werner and Father Josef had seen many battles and each had received medals for their bravery while in combat. After the war Werner became a farmer, and Father Josef entered the priesthood. They had been best of friends for many years.

The strong man contest was Father Josef and Werner's favorite oberfest event. Kegs of beer were stacked on a small stage where the band would normally play. A keg of beer is round and is considered half the size of a barrel. A keg weighs 11 stone or 160 pounds. A contestant gets underneath the stage with the kegs of beer stacked on top. Using his back, he attempts to lift the stage stacked with kegs of beer until all four legs of the stage are off the ground. Once a contestant is successful, another keg is added and someone else gives it a try. The winner is the man who lifts the stage with the most kegs of beer stacked on top. This event would sometimes go on for an entire day. Werner and Father Josef would challenge each other to enter the strong man contest. Each would say, "Of course, I will do it if you do." Father Josef and Werner were only joking and having fun because even though they had both been very strong men when they were young, they were now much older and could no longer lift a stage stacked with kegs of beer. However, they were still very hardy men who thought themselves as strong as any man who entered the contest.

Hans and Bubi were enjoying the tree-climbing competition. The contest was fast and dangerous. There were many contestants. A contestant, using gaffs strapped to his boot, would climb to the top of a tree while racing an opponent on another tree. A gaff is a spike on a flat piece of metal strapped to a boot. The goal is to race to reach the top of the tree, ring a bell that was attached to the top, and then be the first down the tree. Whoever touches the ground first would win. All young men in Bavaria had at one time or another climbed trees using gaffs.

The forest of Bavaria was beautiful and played an important part in Bavarian life. Trees from the forest were used to build homes, barns, and fires to keep the people warm. To cut a tree down, a climber would climb to the top of a tree and cut sections from top to bottom. This way when the heavy sections would fall, they fell straight down and did not damage other trees. The younger men usually did the job of climbing. It took courage to climb to the top of a very tall tree and strong legs and arms to finish the job. Hans had never been in a tree-climbing competition, but he had climbed many trees while helping his father.

Bubi said, "Hans, you should enter this competition. I know you can win. No one can climb as well as you."

Hans and Bubi had been watching the competition for at least an hour. Hans was full of passion to enter, but still he hesitated. Again Bubi said, "Hans, no one can climb as fast as you. You are the best tree climber in Bavaria."

Hans looked at Bubi and took a deep breath. He decided it was time to see if he was indeed the best tree climber in Bavaria. Hans went to the booth where contestants entered the contest and added his name. A lady behind the booth handed him a number and said, "They will call your number when it is your turn." Hans returned to the crowd that was watching the competition and stood next to Bubi. He and Bubi looked at each other but did not speak. Bubi knew his older brother would win. Hans gave Bubi a confident smile, but he was a little nervous.

"Number 27," boomed a loud voice over the crowd. This was Hans' number. This was the last tree-climbing competition of the day. He would be competing against the man with the fastest time of the day. If Hans won this competition, he would have the title of "The Best Tree Climber in Bavaria."

Hans handed Bubi his hat. He approached the tree and was handed a pair of gaffs which he strapped to his boots. At the base of the tree, he lifted his left leg and planted a gaff in the trunk. This was the starting position of the race. Looking up, Hans thought the tree was so tall the top appeared to blend with the sky. For the first time, he looked over at his opponent. All of the men who climbed trees were young. Most were in their early twenties. Hans was only sixteen, much younger than his twenty-year-old opponent. Hans' opponent looked at him and said, "Viel Gluck" which means "good luck" in German. With his gaff firmly struck, Hans placed both hands on the side of the tree and waited for the judge to fire his starting gun. The shot was fired, and Hans raced up the tree staring straight up, keeping his eyes focused on the bell that was getting closer and closer. Hans was strong, and with each powerful push, his body lunged upward. Just as he was reaching up to hit the bell, a loud ring filled the air. It was not his bell. His opponent had made it to the top of the tree seconds before him. Hans grabbed the rope hanging from his bell and gave it a hard tug. The bell rang out, and Hans started down the tree knowing his opponent was seconds ahead of him. Using gaffs makes coming down a tree more difficult than climbing up a tree. Hans was almost leaping down the tree using his gaffs to only barely slow his speed. He no longer knew if he was ahead or behind. Hans dared not turn his head and waste precious seconds to look at his opponent. He could hear the cheering of the crowd grow louder and louder as the ground came closer. Hans was making record time. He continued to make leap after leap downward. Then suddenly he struck the tree with his gaffs, but the gaffs did not hold. He began to fall to the ground with increasing speed. He could not get his gaffs to stick. Each time he attempted to use his gaffs, they bounced off the tree. He hugged the tree with his arms as tight as he could, but still he fell even faster. Suddenly things went black. As he slowly opened his eyes, he found himself sitting on the ground at the base of the tree.

Hans' head ached; his arms were bleeding from hugging the tree, but what hurt most was his bottom. Hans' legs had buckled when he reached the ground, and his bottom hit so hard that it briefly knocked him unconscious. Bubi, his father, and Father Josef were standing above him. Bubi was screaming with excitement, "You won, you won!"

Hans' father had a very worried look on his face and knelt down beside him. Placing a firm hand on his shoulder, he asked, "How are you, my boy? Are you alright?"

"Yes, Father," Hans managed to say in a soft voice. Father Josef took

Hans by one arm, and Werner took his son by the other. Together they gently lifted him to his feet. Hans began to slowly walk around with the help of the two men holding each arm. Bubi was jumping around yelling to anyone who would listen that his brother was the greatest tree climber in Bavaria. Bubi did not notice Hans' pitiful physical condition.

A few minutes later, Hans had regained much of his strength and was feeling better. His bottom was sore, but he could walk, and his head ached only slightly. He had always been a careful climber. This was the first time he had ever taken a fall. Most of the spectators watching the event believed he had made that final leap on purpose. They walked by, slapped him on the back, and congratulated him on winning. Some would even say, "Hans, that was a daring leap you made. Not many would have the courage to do that." Hans only looked at them with a confused smile.

Werner and Father Josef were still standing near, softly chatting with each other. Occasionally they would look at Hans to see if his condition was improving. Hans walked over to his father and said, "How did you know that I had entered the tree-climbing contest?"

His father answered, "I didn't. Josef and I were looking for you and Bubi. Your mother and sister have already left the festival. Now, we must leave and return home. If you are unable to walk, Josef has his horse and cart. You can ride home with him."

Hans knew his father only addressed Father Josef simply as "Josef" when something serious was on his mind. Werner and Father Josef had been through many things in life together. They were more than friends. Their loyalty for each other was as strong as the bond between any two brothers. It was not strange to Hans that his father referred to Father Josef as "Josef," just as it would not be strange if he became a priest and Bubi still addressed him as Hans. Hans said, "Father, what is wrong? Why are we leaving the festival?"

His father said, "The SS are here, and we must leave immediately.

They are looking for soldiers for Hitler's army. Can you walk, or do you want to ride with Josef?" Hans would have rather ridden in the cart with Father Josef, but he did not want his father to think he was hurt. He turned to his father and said, "There is not a problem. I can walk."

The SS, which stands for Schutzstaffel and means "protective shield" in German, were special soldiers devoted to the National Socialist Party. The National Socialist Party was known to the rest of the world as Nazis. Their job was to protect Nazi rallies and break up the meetings of any party that did not agree with them. The German people were very afraid of the SS. They were known for their brutality.

The National Socialists were known to the people of Bavaria as "The Party." They had taken over Germany by violence and destroyed anyone who was against them. Once the Nazis seized control of the German government, their leader, Adolf Hitler, outlawed all elections and became dictator of Germany. A dictator is someone with complete control of the government.

Hans' mother and father wanted no part of the Nazis. The Nazis were conscripting young men as young as fourteen into the military. Conscript means to force someone to join the military. Hans' mother and father, along with Father Josef, knew the SS were at Oktoberfest only for one reason: to find young men to force into the military.

Werner, Hans and Bubi hiked across the countryside and soon arrived back at their farm. Eva and Hiya were waiting for them. Father Josef took the longer route by road and arrived shortly after Werner and the boys. He remained sitting on the cart as Werner and Eva approached. Father Josef looked very somber and did not speak. He knew the decision that Werner and Eva had to make would probably change their lives forever.

Father Josef ran a Catholic boarding school where monks in their brown robes taught classes. The school was for boys who had no mother or father. The Catholic Church was under attack by Hitler, but monks and priests were still allowed to run schools and conduct Mass for people of their faith. Mass is also known as Eucharist and is when people gather in the church to worship. The only place Hans and Bubi would be safe was at the Catholic boarding school. Werner and Eva knew the safety the school offered Hans and Bubi was only temporary, but it was safer than their farm. The SS could arrive at their farm at any time and take the boys away. The next day Hans and Bubi would trade their knickers and woolen knee socks for the school uniform worn at Father Josef's boarding school.

It was decided by Hans' mother that while at the school, Hans would study to be a priest and Bubi an engineer. Hans and Bubi's mother had been the only teacher they had ever known. She had been a good teacher. She taught all of her children reading, writing, math and science. Up until now Father Josef had only taught them Latin one day per week. The school was several kilometers from where Hans and Bubi lived on their farm. The farm was their home, and they did not want to leave, but it was no longer safe for them to stay on the farm. Hans and Bubi got on Father Josef's cart and waved good-bye to their mother, father and sister.

Six months later, the Vatican secretly wrote a letter to the priests across Germany. The Vatican is located in Rome, Italy. It is the religious center of the Catholic Church. The letter said that National Socialism (The Nazi Party) was an evil religion. It was against every man's right to be equal and free. The letter went on to say the leader of the Party (Hitler) was insane. Hitler found out about the letter and became very angry. He put many monks and priests in prison and destroyed many Catholic churches.

The door to Hans and Bubi's small room at the boarding school opened. Father Josef was standing in the doorway. The priest was dressed in a white shirt and mountaineering pants instead of his black robe and flat-brimmed hat. He still wore his large wooden cross. Hans and Bubi were sitting on the edge of their beds getting ready to attend their first class of the day. Father Josef was not smiling. "Do not get up for a moment, boys. I have something I must tell you," he said. Hans sat there frozen. Something must have happened to his mother or father. Bubi looked over at Hans and became very afraid. With tears running down his cheeks, Father Josef said, "We must close the school. You are no longer safe here." He took a deep breath and said, "Hitler has made war with Poland. The SS will be here soon. They are raiding the schools for boys to force them into the Nazi army. Hurry, boys, and gather your things. Your mother, father and sister are waiting. I have made arrangements for you to travel to your new home in Switzerland."

Hans asked, "What about you? Are you not coming with us?" Both Hans and Bubi were very close to Father Josef. He had been like a member of the family.

Father Josef walked over to Hans and lifted him to his feet. Placing his hands on the boy's shoulders, he said, "My work is not finished. There are others that I must help. I will be going to Poland. Do not worry. It is in God's hands."

Hans and his family were among 114,000 Germans who moved out of Germany, fleeing government oppression by the Nazi Party in the months leading to World War II; most never returned.

CHAPTER III
Cubby Leaves the Forest

Cubby awoke in a small underground opening just big enough for a tiny bear cub to enter. The sun had just started to rise. He was afraid and hungry. Cubby was afraid to leave the small cave but just as afraid to stay. Somehow he knew his mother would not be coming to find him. When the sun started to get higher in the sky, he decided it was time to leave the cave and continue running. He had no idea where he was running to, but something in the forest had taken his mother, and his instincts told him he had to get away from that unseen danger.

On the first day of his journey, Cubby recognized much of the forest. His mother's territory in the forest was large. Cubby had roamed over this area many times with his mother in search of food, but now the air was fueled with danger. He knew he had to leave.

Cubby's run turned into a trot and then into a slow walk. He was getting very tired and very hungry. Things began to look different. The air smelled different. It was dry and felt hot. Up ahead there were hills as far as Cubby could see but no forest. Cubby had never seen land with no trees.

In Iran shepherds graze their sheep and cattle in the forest and grass areas until there is nothing left. The shepherds move on to other areas and do the same. These people are called "nomads." The land they leave begins to erode because there is no plant life to provide nutrients for the soil. The forest turns into a desert.

The desert did not look very inviting to Cubby, but the forest was full of danger. So with a heavy sigh, he began to walk into the desert, turning around one last time to say goodbye to his mother and his forest home.

Cubby found walking in the sand much different than walking in the forest. It was much harder to walk in the sand. There were no trees to provide shade, and the sun high up in the sky was burning down with tremendous heat. Cubby's hunger was great, but his need for water became overwhelming. When the sun began to set, Cubby could go no farther. He curled up in a ball with his nose tucked under his paw and went to sleep. When bears sleep, the rate of their heartbeat slows down, and their body uses very little energy. Because of this unique ability that bears have to conserve energy, Cubby was able to survive the night.

The next morning when the sun appeared above the horizon, a boy from a nomadic tribe was wandering in the desert looking for stray sheep. He saw something in the sand that looked odd and out of place. The boy walked closer to see what it was. The young boy discovered a small bear cub curled up in a ball fast asleep. At first he thought the cub was dead, but as he observed more closely, he saw that the cub was gently breathing. He reached down and picked up the tiny bear cub and held him in his arms. Cubby was so exhausted from the lack of food and water, he remained asleep.

The boy was carrying a sack that contained some food and a tiny jug of water. He emptied the sack and carefully put Cubby into the sack. "This will be a wonderful thing to show my family and the other children of my tribe," he thought. The boy tucked the food and water into his robe, put the sack with Cubby inside over his shoulder, and headed back to camp to show everyone what he had found.

The nomads in Iran wear long, flowing woolen robes called sufs (pronounced soof). In ancient times Iran was called Persia, and the Persian people were famous for their garments made from sheep's wool. Egyptian people refined this process and made a finer cut of wool called cashmere. These garments were ideal for the dry, desert climate. They provided shields from the sun and allowed airflow over the body which helped prevent dehydration. Sufs have been worn by nomads in the desert for centuries.

Our young boy's name was Amin. He was eager to reach camp. His tribe was called Bedouins. The word Bedouin in Arabic means "desert people." Bedouins raise cattle, goats and sheep and are considered pastoral people because they shepherd their flocks. Amin had been a trusted shepherd for two full years. He was now sixteen.

A shepherd is extremely important to the tribe and the job is sometimes quite dangerous. In the Iranian desert, predators, such as tigers and leopards, roam many miles from the forest in search of food. The flocks that the shepherds watch are easy prey for the large cats. It is the job of the shepherd to protect the flock at all times. The shepherd's only weapon is a long, thick pole called a staff. He must be brave and protect his flock at all cost, even with his life.

Amin had walked many miles in search of sheep that were separated from the flock. How far he had gone he was not really sure. His father had told him to return to camp before sundown. The sun was now beginning to set in the horizon, and camp was nowhere in sight. He stopped for a moment and lowered the bag that contained Cubby to the ground. Taking out the small water jug, he drank the last of his water.

The difference between day and night in the desert can be extreme. The day time is very hot; however, the night becomes bitterly cold. There is little moisture in the desert to form any cloud coverage. Clouds hold in the heat and keep the land warm at night. In the desert there are no clouds, so the heat escapes at night, and the temperature can drop 21 degrees Celsius (70 degrees Fahrenheit) in a matter of hours. Amin knew if he did not make it to camp before nightfall, he would have to find some way to protect himself from the cold. He had his suf that would help keep him warm, but he needed more. Amin would have to make his own shelter. He began to dig with his hands in the soft sand.

After a lot of effort, he had dug a hole large enough for himself and his new friend Cubby. Cubby was still fast asleep in the sack. Amin lay in the hole and placed the sack by his side. He covered himself and Cubby with sand, leaving just a small portion of his head exposed.

The normally taciturn (inclined to silence) night came, but soon afterwards a resounding (loud and strong) wind began to disturb the quietness of the desert. The wind soon produced such a storm that sand filled the air like a blanket. Amin had his suf wrapped around his head and face with only a small opening for his eyes. He had many hours ahead of him before the sun would appear, and the wind would cease. Sleep would be impossible. Trying to stay calm was the only task at hand. Amin knew that panic in the desert would mean certain death.

After several hours of tormenting wind, sand and cold, Amin heard a faint bellow. No, it could not have been a bellow, for that is the sound a camel would make. A camel would not be roaming the desert in such a sandstorm. Amin knew during sandstorms camels kneel on all fours and hug closely to the ground until the storm has passed. There it was again, except this time it was more like a roar. Camels roar when they are angry or looking for a lost calf. A calf is what baby camels are called. A calf can recognize the unique sound of its mother no matter how many camels are around. In the desert a calf can hear its mother's roar several miles away. A camel's roar is as loud as the roar of a male lion. Amin began to listen very intently. Another roar echoed, and it was getting closer. Could his ears be deceiving him? Was there really a camel in the dark of night, braving such a menacing (threatening) storm the like of which has made entire armies disappear? The desert always buries its dead, sometimes before they are dead.

Camels are well-equipped for the sandstorms of the desert. They have three eyelids. The upper and lower eyelids have long eyelashes that help keep out the sand and filter the sun. The third eyelid is thin and transparent. It moves from side to side like a windshield wiper. The camel's ears are lined with thick fur which also keeps out the sand.

If it was a camel, and Amin's ears were not playing tricks on him, it had to be a camel from his tribe's camp. The camel would know how to get back to camp even in the dark of night and the worst of sandstorms. But it made no sense; a camel simply could not be here. If there was a camel and Amin remained in the hole any longer, the camel could go right past him. However, if there was no camel and he left the safety of the hole, once he was exposed to the wind and sand, he would never survive.

Amin made a decision and decided to make his move. He pushed back the sand and climbed to his feet, bent over at the waist and leaned into the wind, trying with all his power to maintain his balance. As he strained to look from the small opening of his suf, a huge face appeared in front of him. It was the face of a camel. He grabbed the camel around the head and held on with all of his might.

Suddenly he realized that there was a rider on the camel. He was in the saddle on the camel's back but bent over at the waist with his arms wrapped around the camel's neck. The camel went down on all fours, and his belly was flat with the desert. The man began to climb off the camel, and he took Amin by the arm. He pulled him by his side, and they both lay behind the camel. The camel's huge body was blocking the brunt of the storm. Amin knew this man; it was his father.

After a very long time, the wind began to cease, and the dark sky was filled with bright stars. With a feeling of comfort and safety, Amin drifted off to sleep lying by his father up against the camel. As the sun began to rise, Amin opened his eyes. Had this all been a crazy dream? He could feel the body of the camel next to his, but he was alone. Where was his father? He jumped to his feet and saw his father standing ten feet away. "Ah, Amin, you have returned from the dead. Come, I have food and water for you," said his father. Amin walked over to where his father was standing and took the goat skin container that held the water and began to drink. His father then offered Amin some date fruit bread which Amin took immediately and began to rapidly eat.

His father said, "How do you feel? Do you feel well enough to start back to camp?"

Amin nodded his head, and then he said, "Father, how did you know I was in trouble, and how did you find me?"

His father said, "The sky told me there was going to be a storm, and all of your sheep found their way home without you. You are a good shepherd, Amin, and you would never leave your sheep unless you were in trouble."

Amin said, "Father, I came into the desert to look for stray sheep, and the storm came up before I…" Amin stopped in mid-sentence. "Oh no! Where is my bear?" He ran to the area where he had dug the hole to survive the night. Dropping down to his knees, he began to dig ferociously. His hands struck the sack, and Amin pulled it free of the sand. He opened it and looked inside. Cubby was still curled up in a ball and was peeking out above his paw. "He is alive!" said Amin. "Father, look at what I have found. A tiny bear cub. I found him lying in the sand and he is still alive. Look, Father, look!" said Amin.

Amin's father stared at him, and his expression became stern and angry. "Come, Amin, we must get back to camp. Bring the bear if you wish. He will make a good meal. It has been a very long time since your mother has made bear stew," said his father. Amin was struck with horror. He had never heard of bear stew, but Amin knew his father was not one to joke about such things. Amin put Cubby back in the sack, placed it over his shoulder, and climbed on the camel behind his father. After he and his father were safely on the camel, his father commanded the camel to rise. The camel slowly stood to its feet, and they headed back to camp.

Once back at camp, Amin was greeted with great joy by his mother and sisters. He was surprised his father did not share in the occasion. After his mother and sisters gave a sigh of relief, knowing he was safe, his mother said, "Amin, go and find your father. There is something wrong. He did not look well when you and he arrived."

Amin went to the area where the camels were kept and saw his father sitting on the sand with his legs crossed. He walked over to his father and asked, "Father, are you angry with me?" Amin's father looked up at him and asked him to sit. Amin sat down and looked at his father with questioning eyes.

His father said, "Amin, what you did was foolish. You risked your life and our herd to save that bear, which is only going to be a good meal for us. If you had not tried to carry the extra weight of that bear, you could have easily made it back to camp with the sheep long before the storm. Instead, you risked everything, including your life, for that bear. I am greatly disappointed in your judgment."

Amin lowered his head and stared at the sand. He knew it was useless to try to change his father's mind by offering any type of explanation.

After several minutes of silence, his father said, "Go to your mother. Perhaps you can help your sisters. Men with good judgment are needed for shepherd's work." Amin got to his feet and walked back to the tent.

When he entered the tent, he asked, "Mother, where is my sack?" His mother looked over her shoulder where the sack lay in the corner of the tent. Amin went and knelt beside the sack and opened it to find Cubby still curled in a ball. Reaching inside with both hands, Amin lifted Cubby out of the sack. He turned to his mother and said, "Mother, can I have some food for my bear? I do not know how long it has been since he has had food or water, and he must have something to eat and drink or he will die." Amin had several sisters who were intently watching all that was taking place. His mother suddenly had a look of disgust on her face. She understood why Amin's father was angry. She turned her back to him and left the tent.

As soon as his mother had left the tent, Amin's sisters ran and got a jug of honey and a goat skin of water. They rushed over to Amin and handed him the honey and water. Amin stuck his finger in the honey and rubbed it on Cubby's lips. Cubby began to suck Amin's finger until all the honey was gone. The goat skin had a round mouthpiece on the end, and Amin stuck it in Cubby's mouth. Cubby began to suck the water from the goat skin bag until it was completely gone. Amin continued to stick his finger in the honey and into Cubby's mouth until all the honey was gone. Cubby began to climb on Amin and walk around the tent. Cubby did not know what to make of his new surroundings. After having some honey and water, his energy was renewed, but he was still afraid. Amin picked Cubby up in his arms and held him close to his chest. They remained that way for the rest of the day and into the night. Amin was feeling very dejected, and Cubby felt very afraid. Together they gave each other comfort.

The next morning Amin put a rope around Cubby's neck and started walking around the camp with Cubby following close behind. He saw his father and other men of the tribe cutting wool from the sheep.

Amin walked over to his father and said, "Father, I am sorry that I have disappointed you. It was not intentional. I only wanted to save this bear from dying in the desert. I thought he would make a great pet, and my sisters and other children would enjoy playing with him in the camp."

Amin's father stopped what he was doing and went over to where Amin was standing. The other men of the tribe went on working, pretending not to pay any attention to Amin and his father. There were many children in the camp, and they began to gather around Amin and the funny new creature Amin had tied to a rope. The children were laughing and calling out to Cubby to do tricks and to come to them.

Amin looked around and said, "You see, Father, all the children love my bear. No one has ever had a bear before. I am the first. I will train him to help me with tending the sheep." His father looked at him again with that stern look that told Amin his father was not happy.

Amin's father said, "Go tie that bear to the post where the camels are tied and come back. I want to talk with you." Amin did as his father instructed.

Amin and his father walked over to an area where they could be in private, and they both sat down in the sand and crossed their legs. Amin's father said, "You know nothing about bears. They are not like the tiger that will come out of the forest and kill our sheep and then return to the forest. I have seen what a bear can do. This bear will not remain small. He will grow as big as a tent. His appetite will become great. When we cannot feed him he will eat our sheep, our cattle, and maybe even us. Once we hunted bears for their hides and meat, but they became too few to hunt, so we stopped. Bears did not go into the desert, so they were no threat to us. Now you bring one into our camp. Your mother wants this bear to eat. That is what we should do. He has no mother, or he would not have been alone. If you turn him loose, he will die in the desert. If he returns to the forest, hunters will hunt him for his fur. There is now a big price paid for bear fur, even a small bear's fur. Either way, he will not live long. It is better that we kill him now than wait until he eats all our food and gets large enough to kill our cattle and maybe us."

Amin was heartbroken. He had never dreamed that after all his bear had been through that he would be killed by Amin's own tribe and become bear stew.

Amin appealed to his father. He said, "Father, please grant me this one request, and I will forever be loyal to your wishes. I know my bear is doomed, but allow me to return him to the desert and set him free. I would rather cut out my heart than kill this bear and give him to mother to make stew." Amin's father's face began to show empathy for his son. Amin looked at his father and had hope. However, there was a culture within the tribe, and traditions were rarely broken. Amin's father was respected among the tribal men and to let this bear go would be a sign of weakness. However, Amin's father did the unthinkable. He told Amin, "Go, take the bear into the desert. But I warn you, if you come back with him, he will be food on our table and a small rug for your mother. Leave early tomorrow morning, and be back before sunset." Amin was overjoyed. He felt as if the weight of ten thousand camels had been taken off his shoulders.

The next morning, Amin gathered several date cakes, a goat skin of water, and a small jug of honey. He started his journey before the sun came up. Amin knew his bear had only escaped death temporarily. It would take a miracle for his bear to survive in the desert. But miracles do happen. Did not his father find him in the dead of night in a blinding storm when he had no food or water? Was that not a miracle?

Yes, my dear readers, Cubby had escaped death once again—but for how long? We shall return to Cubby's saga shortly, but at present it is imperative (necessary) we find Father Josef. He has not fared well in his efforts to aid the Polish people.

CHAPTER IV

Escape from the Siberian Gulags

The war between Germany and Poland did not last long. The German army was much better equipped and had more soldiers than the Polish forces. Germany had also entered into a secret agreement with the Soviet Union, and they joined together in the attack against Poland. It was agreed that Germany would attack Poland from the west, and the Soviet Union would attack Poland from the east. In a few short weeks, Poland surrendered.

Some of the captured Polish soldiers were sent to German prison camps. Others were sent to Siberia in the Soviet Union and were placed in prison camps called gulags. Father Josef had joined the Polish army as a chaplain. A chaplain in the military does not fight the enemy during war, but they do sometimes go on the battlefield. They help wounded soldiers and give comfort to others by praying for their safety and listening to them talk about their fears and loved ones left behind. Father Josef was part of the Polish army who were prisoners of the Soviet Union. He was being sent to the gulags in Siberia. Gulags were prison camps where prisoners were used as slave labor. They worked in coal and copper mines and lived in extremely cold weather conditions. The prisoners were fed only bread and occasionally a soup made of anything the guards did not want to eat. At night they slept in unheated wooden buildings called barracks. Many prisoners died as a result of their cruel treatment.

Siberia is a very large territory. It makes up 77 percent of the Soviet Union, which today is known as Russia. In 1904, many years before our story takes place, a railroad called the Trans-Siberian Railroad was built in the southern part of Siberia. It ran all the way to Moscow, the capital of the Soviet Union. Today, the Trans-Siberian Railroad is still the longest railway line in the world. It is 9,441 km (5,867 miles) long. If a similar railroad were built in the United States, it would reach all the way across the country and all the way back, and there would still be track left over. The winters in southern Siberia are brutally cold. The average temperature is -25 degrees C (-13 degrees F). My word, my dear readers, it is warmer in your kitchen freezer!

The agreement between the Nazi leader, Adolf Hitler, and the Soviet Union's leader, Joseph Stalin, lasted about two years. Hitler took Stalin totally by surprise and attacked the Soviet Union. The attack was particularly bad for the people in the Soviet Union because they were starving. Their food supplies had always been low, but now because of an extremely cold winter, the food supplies were even lower than normal. Now Stalin had a war with Germany on his hands and very little food to feed his army. That left nothing for the Polish prisoners in his gulags.

Then Stalin had an idea. He could use those Polish prisoners. Stalin told them they would be released if they agreed to join the Soviet army. Some of the Polish soldiers joined the Soviets; others refused. Stalin said those who refused would face certain death either by execution or starvation. What Stalin did not know was that those who refused had decided to escape to Africa.

The Polish soldiers had heard the British were fighting the Germans in Africa. They wanted to join the British and fight against the Germans who had attacked their homeland, but to escape meant traveling over the snow-covered mountains of Siberia and across the Iranian desert. If you will remember, my dear readers, the Iranian desert is where we left our friends, Amin and Cubby. Many of the soldiers thought the journey would be impossible; however, these were determined men, and sometimes determined men do the impossible.

Father Josef took a deep breath and inhaled the fresh air of the Bavarian mountains. He could see the beautiful forest as he looked out the window of his room at the boarding school. He could hear the young boys playing in the courtyard just outside his room. Father Josef got up from his chair and moved toward the door to go outside. He had decided to take a stroll around the grounds of the school. Perhaps he would visit a nearby town and have a glass of beer and a bratwurst. A bratwurst is a fried sausage. In German 'brat' means to fry and 'wurst' means sausage. When Father Josef reached for the door, suddenly someone was shaking him and calling his name. "Father Josef, Father Josef!" the voice cried. He opened his eyes, and Peter was standing beside his bed. Peter was a Polish soldier that had been captured by the Soviets at the same time as Father Josef. It had all been a dream. Father Josef was not in Bavaria. He awoke in the Siberian gulag.

Peter said, "Father Josef, some of us have decided not to join the Soviets. We are going to escape to Africa and fight the Nazis with the British. We will be leaving before sunup. I want to say goodbye and to ask that you pray for our safety."

Father Josef sat up on the side of the small bed. He looked at Peter and said, "Yes, my son, I will pray for your safety, but why was I not told about this before?"

Peter said, "Father, if our plan is discovered, everyone involved will be shot. We did not want to put your life at risk."

Father Josef looked at Peter and said, "When do we leave?"

Peter looked at Father Josef, and his heart filled with joy. During the time the soldiers had spent in the gulags, Father Josef had been a great comfort to many of the prisoners. He had offered them hope when there was none and helped nurse many back to health when they were on death's bed.

Peter said, "Father, you are going to join us? This is wonderful news, Father! It will give the men courage to know you are among us. The men are already waiting. We must leave while it is still dark. The guards are inside the guard shack and will be coming out at the first sign of daylight. We haven't much time."

Father Josef rose from his bed and said, "I am ready. Lead the way, Peter." Father Josef was wearing the same clothing he had been wearing when he was captured. He had worn them night and day for several months. In gulag prison camps, prisoners never removed their clothes for fear of freezing to death.

Peter and Father Josef quickly joined the men in a dark corner of the prison camp. Peter had served with these men as a member of a Polish artillery unit. Artillery units operate large cannons that fire shells that weigh 6 stones (80 pounds) or more and that can travel four kilometers (over two miles). An army uses the artillery to weaken the defense of the enemy so the infantry (foot soldiers) can advance into enemy territory. There were originally 250 men in Peter's artillery unit, but only 80 had survived the gulags.

There was no moon to cast light off the snow. The prisoners had been waiting for just such a night. The darkness would give them some safety and help to prevent them from being discovered by the guards. Earlier several of the soldiers had raided the guards' supply shack and took as many cans of food and as much bread as they could carry. They found large wire cutters that could be used to cut through the fence that surrounded the gulag. Picks, axes and shovels were taken, along with wool blankets to help them survive the cold. These supplies were far from everything they needed, but they would risk the escape just the same. The men all stayed close and silent. Each prisoner looked at the face of another knowing the odds were badly against them. It was an effort to give confidence to their fellow prisoner that the escape would be successful. These men were prisoners, but they were also soldiers. A soldier's duty when captured was to escape no matter how bad the odds. It was time.

Peter held his hand in the air and made a scissor-cutting motion with two of his fingers. From the group, two men moved toward the fence. Everyone watched as the men quietly cut a large hole in the fence. Once the task was completed, Peter raised his hand in the air and made a pointing motion toward the fence. Silently the men moved forward. One by one each made their way through the opening. In less than five minutes, all eighty men were on the other side of the fence and moving down the Siberian mountainside.

A Russian guard had been on his way to the supply shack to get food for breakfast. The guard saw the last of the prisoners escaping through the fence. He began yelling, "Oni Ubegayut, Oni Ubegayut!" ("They are escaping!," in Russian). The prisoners could hear the commotion made by the guards running from the guard shacks to their post. A soldier's post is where he goes to do a specific task or job for which he is trained. Within seconds machine gun fire filled the air. The guards could not see the prisoners, so they fired randomly into the darkness. Machine gun bullets hit the ground all around the escaping prisoners. They continued running until they had reached the safety of the forest. The dense forest offered the prisoners protection. The prisoners knew that once the machine guns stopped, the guards would be coming after them on foot. Their bodies were weak from the cold and lack of food, but they must not stop running until they were far away from the gulag.

The guards did not search long for the prisoners. They wanted to return to the comfort of their guard shacks where there were hot stoves to keep them warm. Besides, with the prisoners gone, there would be more food for them. The guards knew the prisoners could never survive in the Siberian forest.

The prisoners ran through the forest for hours. They had reached the bottom of the mountain and could go no farther. Their hands and feet were numb from the cold. They were tired and weak, but they were free; for now that was enough. The men could think of themselves as soldiers again instead of prisoners in the gulags.

The soldiers gathered at the base of a mountain range called the Caucasus. The Caucasus mountain range has the highest peak in Europe. It is 5,642 meters (18,510 feet) to the top of the highest peak.

That is over three miles high! The southern part of the mountain range is called the Transcaucasus Mountains (Transcaucasus means South Caucasus). It is here we find Peter and the other soldiers. They would have to find a way to cross the Caucasus to reach the Caspian Sea and then journey into Iran. Once they reached Iran, they would have to cross the Iranian desert before they could join the British in Africa. The journey would have been difficult for a well-equipped army with plenty of supplies, but for the tired and hungry soldiers that lay at the bottom of the mountain, it seemed like a wild, impossible dream.

Peter asked for a volunteer to count the soldiers. He needed to know how many men had survived the escape. Father Josef got to his feet and said, "I will count the men." He began to move about, noticing the condition of each soldier as he counted. Peter asked for all the supplies to be brought forward so a ration (daily allowance) could be established for each soldier. Father Josef returned and said to Peter, "We have sixty-four remaining." During the escape sixteen men had been killed. The remaining sixty-four men hardly looked like human beings. Ice had formed in their beards and hair. Their faces showed only a glint (tiny light) of life, and their bodies were thin from the lack of food. Peter asked for volunteers to help distribute the food rations. Normally a soldier would be assigned to a job instead of being asked to volunteer. However, they were all in such poor condition, it was impossible to know which of the soldiers had the physical strength to help. Aleksy, Fabian, Dominik, and Henryk came forward. They distributed the food among the men, and the remainder was divided into a daily ration for their journey.

After some food and rest, Peter, Aleksy, Fabian, Dominik, and Henryk gathered and discussed a plan to cross the Transcaucasus Mountains. Father Josef spent his time helping the soldiers. The men knew that in the mountains and valleys, there were mountain sheep, ibex (wild goats), and bison which could be trapped for food.

You may wonder what a bison looks like. The American buffalo is a bison. It is not really a buffalo. French explorers in North America called them "les boeufs" which means oxen or cattle. Later English-speaking settlers thought the French were calling the bison a "buffalo" and the name stuck. A bison weighs 143 stone (2,000 pounds) and can run forty miles per hour. That is faster than a horse, tiger or bear can run. Bison are usually gentle animals that travel in herds. A herd is about 100 bison that live, feed and travel together. Bison do not eat meat. They are vegetarians. If the soldiers could get food and manage not to freeze to death, their goal of reaching Africa just might be possible. However, where there was food for the soldiers, there was food for the wolves and snow leopards. Wolves and snow leopards only eat meat. They are not picky about which meat they eat when hungry. A soldier would taste just as good as an ibex.

The Transcaucasus Mountains are home to the snow leopards and the Siberian gray wolf. Snow leopards weigh about 8 stone (120 pounds). Like all cats, they are carnivores. They are crepuscular hunters which means they hunt in the early morning or late afternoon. They have gray fur with dark blotches and rings. A snow leopard is about 130 cm (50 inches) long. Its tail is as long as its body. They use their tails for balance when climbing and wrap it around their body to keep warm when resting. Their sense of smell is so keen they can smell an animal's tracks in the snow. Unlike other cats their eyes are pale green. Snow leopards can see six times better than a human. If you could see that well, it would mean your teacher could just open a book at the front of the classroom and hold it up, and you would be able to easily read it from the back row. Snow leopards do not just see well, they have a large chest and incredibly strong shoulders. They can kill animals five times their size.

The Siberian gray wolf has a thick coat of gray fur. Their eyes are pale blue. The gray wolf weighs 9 stone, (130 pounds). In comparison, the friendly Labrador, a popular family dog, typically weighs 4 stone (65 pounds). It is considered a large dog, yet it is only half the size of a gray wolf. Wolves travel in packs. A pack usually consists of six to seven wolves. They hunt constantly. When the wolves attack their prey, it is always as a pack. They silently form a circle around the prey before attacking. This prevents their prey from being able to escape, since they are surrounded in every direction. Wolves can take down and kill a full-grown bison in a matter of minutes.

The soldiers decided that scouts should be sent ahead of the group to find the best routes. Aleksy and Henryk volunteered to be the group's scouts. A detail (small group) was organized to cut small tree limbs and sharpen them into spears for weapons.

Fire was needed to keep the men warm and to keep the dangerous snow leopards and wolves away. Snow leopards and wolves are afraid of fire. To make a fire in the snow would sound impossible to some, but survival often depends on doing the impossible.

An abundance of dead trees are found in the forest. The bark of dead trees is dry and can easily be stripped from the trees in large pieces. Some of the dead tree limbs fall and are buried beneath the snow. Snow in high altitudes is actually very dry. The wood buried beneath the snow remains fairly dry as well. Digging beneath the snow, the soldiers gathered a supply of wood and also dead grass that would quickly dry when exposed to the air. They searched for a rock called pyrite. Pyrite rock is plentiful in the mountains. Pyrite is also called "fool's gold" because crystals and iron trapped in the rock make it shine like gold.

To start a fire, the soldiers trampled the snow down until they had created a small, circular wall to keep out the wind. Then they placed the tree bark inside the circle. Scraping the lint (loose fabric) from their blankets and clothes, they made a small ball of wool and placed it on the bark. The soldiers struck two pyrite rocks together to release sulfur and small flakes of iron that were trapped in the rock. The sulfur ignites with oxygen in the air and creates a spark. The spark heats the iron flakes, and they turn red hot. The red hot iron flakes fall on the lint and the lint begins to burn. By gently blowing on the burning ball of lint the flame spreads and then dry grass is added. Once the grass is burning, larger pieces of wood are added until a large fire is created keeping the soldiers warm and the dangerous animals away. The soldiers took burning pieces of wood from their first fire and started others. They divided up into small groups and made camps around each new fire.

The next morning Aleksy and Henryk each took a spear, a ration of food, pieces of pyrite rock and a blanket. After bidding the other men goodbye, they headed south. They agreed to separate but to stay in sight of each other. At night they would meet and make camp until the first sign of daylight. They hiked through the mountains and valleys, leaving marks on the rocks and signs made of dead wood for the soldiers to follow. Both men were excellent scouts. They were skilled trappers and often set traps to catch game for the soldiers who were following a day or two behind.

The soldiers were making good progress traveling through Siberia. They had food to eat, more than they had ever had in the gulags, and fire to keep them warm at night. Peter organized the men into groups of ten to twelve soldiers each. At night each group would have their own camp. Members of the group would take turns all through the night adding wood to the fire and being on the lookout for danger. It was in this manner the soldiers were able to escape Siberia and reach the Caspian Sea.

My dear readers, you may be wondering about our friends, Amin and Cubby. We shall visit them soon, but first we must discover how the soldiers crossed the Caspian Sea.

CHAPTER V

Across the Caspian Sea to the Iranian Desert

Many countries border the Caspian Sea. It is the largest enclosed body of water on Earth. It is actually not a sea but a giant lake. From north to south, it spans 1,000 kilometers (600 miles). Many different types of fish and plant life live in the Caspian Sea. Ninety percent of all fish known as sturgeons are found in the Caspian Sea.

The beluga sturgeon is the largest freshwater fish in the world. It can weigh 1,571 kg (3,460 pounds) and sometimes exceed 5m (16ft) in length. It is almost the size of the great white shark. The beluga sturgeon is famous worldwide for their roe (eggs) called caviar. For over 100 years, kings and queens have considered beluga caviar a delicacy. Beluga is Russian for white. It is considered the most expensive food on earth. Beluga caviar costs between $7,000 and $10,000 for 1kg (2.2 pounds) or $200 to $300 per ounce. Beluga sturgeon can live to be 118 years old.

A fishing industry for the sturgeons, brown trout, white salmon, mullet, herring, carp, crayfish and shrimp stretches across the Caspian Sea from the coast of Russia to the coast of Iran. It was on the Caspian Sea, along the coast of Russia, that Aleksy and Henryk materialized like two ghosts from the grave. They had survived their journey through the Transcaucasus Mountains, but when they reached the beach of the Caspian Sea, their legs gave way, and they fell with their faces in the sand.

Aleksy and Henryk had emerged from the mountains within two kilometers (a little over one mile) from a fishing village. Two young boys from the village were fishing along the beach with their fishing nets. One of the boys saw the two lifeless figures on the beach.

One boy said to the other boy, "Look, what is that on the beach?"

The other boy looked in the direction his friend was pointing and said, "It looks like two dead men." Without speaking the two boys began to move closer to the bodies on the beach. The boys were no strangers to dead bodies. The weather on the Caspian Sea changes very quickly. It was not unusual for a fishing boat to be caught in a sudden storm many miles from shore. During the storms, sometimes a fisherman would fall overboard and later wash up on the shore. Lately the weather had been good, and no one from the village was missing. While the boys were slowly moving closer, Aleksy coughed and then made a soft moaning noise. The boys froze in their tracks.

They looked at each other and one said, "They are alive. We should go to the village for help." They dropped their nets on the beach and began to run as fast as their legs would carry them.

The young boys were from a tribe of people known as Caspi. A tribe consists of several families who share the same blood ties and culture. The word Caspi is from ancient Persia which is now called Iran. No one is really sure where the Caspi people originated. There is some mention of them in scrolls found in ancient Egypt, but this could mean they only traveled there for trade instead of originating from ancient Egypt. The Caspian Sea was named after the Caspi people. They have a language that only they speak and understand. There are only about 100 Caspian people in the world today.

The two young boys returned to their village. They ran to a boat where they saw four village fishermen unloading the day's catch of fish. The young boys told the fishermen about finding two men on the beach. They explained how they thought the men were dead until suddenly one of them moved.

One of the fishermen said, "Let's hurry to help these men." The young boys started off down the beach with all four of the fishermen following close behind. When they reached Aleksy and Henryk, they were still lying in the sand. The fishermen carried the pair back to their village and put them in a hut (small house) where the village people stayed when they were sick. A village medicine man was there, and he gave them each a drink whose ingredients were only known to the medicine man. Some of the villagers brought fish for them to eat and goat's milk to drink. The next morning, Aleksy and Henryk were able to stand and walk out of the hut.

When Aleksy and Henryk left the hut, they found villagers gathered outside. Everyone was curious to see the strangers found on the beach. There were village elders among the crowd. Elders are older men of high ranking in the village. One of the elders approached Aleksy and Henryk. The elder began to communicate with the two soldiers. Throughout history travelers of the world have been able to communicate with people who did not speak their language. They communicate by making lexical (expressed) signs with their hands and by facial expressions. The elder pointed to Henryk and then to the mountains with a raised eyebrow. Henryk understood the elder was asking him where they were from. Henryk took a stick and began to draw pictures in the sand. He drew pictures of the prison camp from which they escaped and their journey through the Transcaucasus Mountains. After a while the elder gave Henryk a sign he understood by moving his head up and down. The elder turned and, in the Caspian language, relayed to the crowd what he had learned. Henryk drew pictures of the other soldiers and pointed to the mountains to indicate that they would be arriving soon. The elder moved his head up and down to show he understood.

Next Henryk drew pictures of boats crossing the Caspian Sea to Iran. He asked the elder, by opening his hands with his eyebrows furrowed (gathered), if he would help. The elder again gave the sign that he understood. This time he turned and spoke to the people of the village for several minutes. When he finished, the crowd was silent for a long, tense moment.

Then someone in the crowd yelled, "We must help these men." The crowd cheered their approval. Aleksy and Henryk did not understand the Caspian language, but they knew the people of the village were going to help. They stood facing the cheering crowd with huge smiles on their faces. They had escaped the gulags. Now with the help of the Caspian people, they would make it to Iran. The only thing between them and Africa was their journey across the Iranian desert.

A few days later, the other soldiers found their way out of the mountains. They had followed Aleksy and Henryk's signs and arrived at the same location the scouts had found three days earlier. The soldiers were in somewhat better condition than Aleksy and Henryk had been when they had arrived. Thanks to the traps Aleksy and Henryk had set along the way, the soldiers had more food to eat. It was easier to follow the trail left by the scouts, so they had more time to build warm fires at night. The village people gave the soldiers food and a place to sleep. The climate was much warmer on the coast, and within a few days, they were ready to cross the Caspian Sea to Iran.

The voyage over the Caspian Sea took ten days. For some of the soldiers, it was the first time they had ever been on a boat. Many were seasick the entire voyage. Seasickness is the urge to vomit caused by the motion of the waves. The Caspian fishermen used all ten fishing boats to transport the soldiers to Iran. The boats were built to catch fish not transport soldiers. It was not an easy voyage for the men. The boats were crowded. The soldiers spent most of their days out in the clean fresh air. The area below the deck was very small and with berths (sleeping space) for only four people and a food preparation area. The berths, which looked like hammocks, were sheets of canvas attached by ropes to the boat. The berths were saved for the soldiers with the most severe seasickness.

The boats had one large mast, a mainsail, and a headsail. A mast is a tall, thick pole used to support the boat's sails. The mainsail is the largest sail and is attached to the mast. The headsail is a smaller sail attached to the mast at the top and to the boat at the bottom. A headsail is only used when the boat is traveling leeward. Leeward is an ocean term which means traveling downwind. Windward means traveling upwind. The boats were 10 meters (about 33 feet) long with wide bodies. The bodies were deep and open, so they could carry a lot of fish. The boat design also made the boats very stable in the vast open sea. During a storm waves can reach more than 6 meters (20 feet) high. Compared to traveling through the Transcaucasus Mountains, the soldiers found the Caspian Sea voyage a much easier challenge but a challenge just the same.

When the boats arrived in the port of Pahlavi in Iran, some of the soldiers knelt down along the sandy shoreline and kissed the soil. Dominik and Father Josef were laughing and talking about their journey. They were speaking in Father Josef's native Bavarian German which was very unusual for Father Josef. Father Josef spoke several European languages. However, when speaking with others, he tried to speak with them only in their native language. For the past two years, he had only spoken Polish. Dominik spoke excellent German because his family had lived in Germany before the war. Like so many other Europeans, they had lived in several different countries that were once friendly but were now at war with each other. They were originally from Poland, but Dominik's father had accepted a teaching position at a German university when Dominik was a young boy. The family had moved back to Poland in the early years leading up to Hitler's takeover of Germany.

Soon the Iranian army arrived. Although the Iranian soldiers had guns, the army did not seem aggressive. The Iranian soldiers got out of the trucks with rifles in hand, but the weapons were held close to their chests, a sign in the military that the guns were not intended to be used. There were two officers in the group who did not carry weapons.

Peter approached the officers and asked in Polish, "Do you speak Polish or German?"

One of the Iranian officers replied, "Yes, I understand both Polish and German." Most of the people of Iran speak several languages. Iran has been one of the major trading regions of the world for hundreds of years. Peter explained how he and the other soldiers had escaped the Soviet gulags, and with the help of the Caspian fishermen, they had arrived at the port of Pahlavi. Peter said, "We ask permission to enter your country and be allowed to continue our journey to Africa. I will guarantee the conduct of my men while we are here. We will need some time to prepare to cross the desert, but our stay will be as brief as possible."

The Iranian officer asked, "Why are you going to Africa?"

Peter responded, "To join the British command. We must regain the independence of Poland."

Iran was a neutral country that did not take either side in the war. They had traded with Germany and Russia for many years. The Iranian officer said, "You will be allowed to make camp on the beach but must leave Pahlavi in three weeks. We will help you prepare for your journey to Africa."

All the soldiers had gathered around Peter and the Iranian officer to hear their conversation. Everyone's future depended on the Iranian officer's decision. When the soldiers heard they would be allowed to stay, they expressed a collective sigh of relief. They turned and started back to the fishing boats to thank the Caspian fishermen for all they had done, but they were too late. Silently the Caspian fishermen had set their boats out to sea. The soldiers began waving and cheering to the Caspian fishermen in an effort to show their gratitude for all they had done. In the distance, the soldiers could see the fishermen waving back as they hoisted their sails and quietly disappeared over the horizon.

Over the next several days, the soldiers began to enjoy their new freedom. The Iranian army supplied them with tents and food. Soon the shoreline of Pahlavi looked like a small city of tents. The people of

Pahlavi brought the soldiers clothing and shoes. Never had the soldiers been treated with such kindness. Up until now, their life had been merely a matter of survival.

One day a young woman wearing a long, dark-colored dress was moving among the soldiers. She had a scarf wrapped around her head and neck with the ends of the scarf spread across her shoulders. The young woman was carrying a basket of bread. She held the basket in front of Father Josef to offer him some bread. Father Josef was deep in thought and at first did not notice her. He was sitting on the beach without his shirt or shoes and with his pants legs rolled up to his knees.

When the young woman offered Father Josef bread, he noticed the ring she was wearing. In the ring was an image known as "The Sacred Heart of Jesus." The image is a picture of Jesus with the heart in his chest exposed. Jesus is the central figure of a religion called Christianity. Father Josef recognized this as a scapular ring, a particular type of ring worn by nuns to help remind them to pray. Nuns are a community of Catholic women who live together and make vows (promises) of poverty and obedience to God.

Father Josef could not believe his eyes. He immediately jumped to his feet which caused the young woman to take two or three steps backwards in shock. The young woman did not look Iranian. She looked more European. In Polish Father Josef said, "My name is Father Josef. Are you a nun?" The young woman had a surprised look on her face and did not reply. Father Josef was not sure if she understood what he had said. They stood there staring at each other with expressions of confusion on their faces.

The young woman could tell from the way Father Josef spoke that Polish was not his native language. She did understand some Polish but decided to reply to him in Italian to see if he understood.

She said, "My name is Sister Catherine. You said your name is Father Josef. Are you a Catholic priest?"

Father Josef laughed and in Italian said, "It seems I have surprised you as much as you have surprised me."

Father Josef explained that he had joined the priesthood as a young man in Bavaria and had later run a school for orphaned boys outside Munich. Sister Catherine smiled and said, "Then I am even more surprised to find you here, Father, among these men."

Father Josef understood her bewilderment and said, "God does work in mysterious ways, Sister. Would you have a few minutes to talk before you return to your work?" Sister Catherine smiled and placed her basket on the beach. She and Father Josef sat in the sand and talked for over an hour.

They shared stories of their lives and how they came to be in Iran. The young woman explained that she was from Italy and was a member of the order of the Sisters of Nazareth. The sisters (nuns refer to each other as sisters) had established an orphanage in Pahlavi for children who lost their parents in the war. An orphanage is a home for children who do not have a mother or father. The raging war in Europe had orphaned many children.

When Sister Catherine had finished telling Father Josef about the orphanage and what a blessing the local people had been with all their help, Father Josef asked, "How would I find this orphanage? I would like to visit the children before I leave."

Sister Catherine was delighted. She said, "Yes, Father, please come visit our children's home! My sisters and I have started a school with the orphanage, but we have few books from which to teach. Perhaps you could look at what we have and give us some instructions on how to improve the school."

Sister Catherine then made arrangements to return the next day and take Father Josef to see the home and meet the children.

Sister Catherine and Father Josef stood. Father Josef said, "Until tomorrow then, Sister. God be with you."

Sister Catherine said, "Until tomorrow, Father. God be with you as well." Sister Catherine picked up her basket of bread. She moved from tent to tent offering bread to the soldiers until her basket was empty. Sister Catherine then returned to the orphanage and told her sisters about the priest she had just met. Sister Catherine and Father Josef had met under the most unusual circumstances. It is said, my dear readers, by those who know more than I, "When good people come together, it is always for a good reason."

Peter and the men were busy preparing for their journey across the Iranian desert. Dominik and Fabian had made friends with many of the local fishermen. They were gathering rations of fish jerky. Fish jerky is fish that has been dried in the sun. Fish jerky is safe to eat for over a year after it has been dried. When dried, the salt is retained in the fish which makes it an excellent food for the desert. Salt is essential to the human body.

In the desert a person sweats a lot. Through continuous sweating, the salt levels in the body fall and cause severe headaches and cramping of the muscles. The salt in the fish jerky helps maintain the body's salt levels. Fish jerky is high in nutrition (vitamins and minerals) and weighs very little, so it is easy to carry.

Henryk and Aleksy had made friends with some of the Iranian soldiers. The soldiers were helping Henryk and Aleksy get supplies of canned meat called corned beef. Canned meat can last for forty years. It retains most of its nutrition, but canned meat is heavy and difficult to carry.

The Iranian people gave the soldiers dried fruits, such as dates, figs and raisins. They also gave them honey, pomegranates, bread, wheat, barley, tea and goats. The Iranian people were very generous to the soldiers.

Father Josef received nomad tents from some of the merchants. Tents used by the nomads are made from densely woven goat's hair. A goat's hair tent stays cool in the burning sun during the day and warm when the nights are cold. It rarely rains in the desert, but when it does, it rains a huge amount in a short period of time. Keeping supplies dry is very important. Water will not penetrate (go through) a tent made of goat's hair.

Peter and the other men had to find a way to supply water for the soldiers during their trip. Water was the most important supply that the soldiers needed for their journey. Planning how to carry or transport water across the desert is very complicated because water is heavy. Four liters (about 1 gallon) of water weighs about 4 kilograms (a little over 8 pounds). Peter and the soldiers went to the Iranian people to seek their advice. This is what they learned.

They were told the nomads only travel in the early morning and late afternoon. The soldiers would travel like the nomads. This would reduce the need for water because the men would be staying out of the heat of the midday sun. The need for water depends on the individual. On average a person will need 4 liters of water (about 1 gallon) for every 32 kilometers (20 miles) they travel in the desert, providing they stay out of the extreme heat during the day. When water gets hot, it loses its disinfectants (something that kill germs).

The men were told the best way to travel across the desert was to do as the camels do. A camel knows the best place to store water is in the body. A camel will drink up to 200 liters (53 gallons) of water within five minutes and then be able to go days and even weeks before needing more. The Iranians explained that, like a camel, the men should drink water before they were thirsty. Then they would be carrying water in their bodies which is much easier to transport than carrying it in containers.

Still, the men would need containers. They were told that containers made of animal skins are a good way to carry water. This would help to keep the water cool. Now, to find the water, the soldiers would need to listen carefully because their lives would depend upon it. The methods explained to the soldiers did not guarantee they would find water, but it increased their chances.

One-fifth or 20% of the earth is desert and is also home to about one-sixth (17%) of the earth's population. Out of the thousands of people who have lived in the desert over the last several thousand years, few have died from the lack of water. If the soldiers were careful and traveled as the desert dwellers had for so many years, they would survive the journey. They were especially grateful for the valuable knowledge the Iranian people shared with them.

The following day Sister Catherine met Father Josef on the beach and took him to the orphanage. The two-story building had twenty-seven small bedrooms on the top floor and three large rooms on the bottom floor. The building had been given to the sisters to use for their orphanage by Mohammad Reza, the last Shah of Pahlavi. A shah is the supreme ruler of the state. The Shah was sympathetic to the orphan children and provided them with food and clothing.

Father Josef was delighted to meet the children, and they were delighted to meet him. The sisters showed Father Josef the rooms where they held classes and the books they used. Father Josef spent time looking through the books while making notes as to his thoughts. He walked the grounds of the orphanage and inspected the bedrooms where the children slept. In the evening, he asked to have a meeting with the sisters.

After the children had said their prayers and had gone to bed for the night, the sisters met with Father Josef in one of the large rooms where the children were taught. Father Josef said, "My beloved sisters, you are doing a wonderful job here with the children. You give the children their daily religious instructions, and they are in good health. This is all very good. There is no instruction on mathematics and the sciences because you have no books from which to teach. I understand the children should be taught Latin. All European languages use Latin words, and it will be easier for them to understand other languages. You have done very well, but my advice is to find a way to add these subjects to your school."

The nun in charge of the orphanage was named Mother Superior Mary Teresa. The title "Mother Superior" is given to the nun who is the leader of the nuns. She said, "Father Josef, thank you for visiting the children's home and for sharing your advice about the school. We can teach Latin because it was taught to us by the church as part of our training to become nuns. However, no one here has any knowledge of mathematics or science except what was written in the Holy Scripture (Bible)."

Father Josef had attended the university in Munich when he was a teenage boy. He knew there were very few girls who attended the universities. What little training in mathematics and science that girls received came from their fathers or older brothers who had attended the universities. Even the number of men who had knowledge of mathematics and science was small. Most families did not have the money to send their children to universities. Families that did have the money only sent their boys. Father Josef's parents had been large landowners in Germany. They raised sheep, cattle and pigs. They also sold trees called Bavarian Spruce. The Bavarian Spruce was used to make piano keys and beautiful furniture, but its largest use was to make paper. Father Josef's family sold timber (trees) to paper mills in Austria, and they were considered wealthy people.

Father Josef was the oldest of three boys. His parents had sent him to the university to study medicine. He was in his third year at the university when a war began which was called the "Great War" (WWI). Father Josef left the university and joined the German army. When the war was over, he entered the priesthood for reasons only known to Father Josef. While he attended the university, he had received a very good education in mathematics and many of the sciences. After becoming a priest he put his knowledge to use by opening schools for orphan boys. Now, my dear readers, we know more about this courageous man who devoted his life to helping others.

Father Josef said, "Mother Superior, I will pray tonight for guidance so that I may help you. I will come to visit you again before I leave."

Mother Superior said, "That would be wonderful, Father. Your visit to our children's home has been a blessing. The sisters and I will pray for your safe passage to Africa."

When Father Josef returned to camp, he found the men settling in for the night. It was getting late, and some had already gone to sleep. Fabian was standing on the shoreline staring over the water. It was a full moon, and the moonlight splashed off the sea to light up the night. It was very quiet with only the sound of a few soldiers talking amongst themselves.

Father Josef walked over and stood next to Fabian.

After a few moments, Father Josef asked, "How was your day, my son?"

Fabian did not notice Father Josef had walked up next to him. He turned and said, "It is good to see you, Father. I was just thinking about my childhood on my father's small farm. It was a simple life, but every day I heard laughter in my house. My mother was a great cook, and we had large family meals every night. I have five brothers, and we worked together every day. I am third from the oldest. My father was a very strong man and knew so many things which he taught my brothers and me. I miss them, Father. I wonder if there will ever be a time when I will see them again."

Father Josef put his hand on Fabian's shoulder and said, "Only God knows the answer to that question. But remember this, the love you have in your heart for your family, they also have for you. This will never change. Perhaps one day, you will have a son. You will be a part of his childhood and his memories. Pray for your future, not your past. You are a good man, Fabian. Be God's vessel (ship), and carry goodness into the world. You are young, and there is still much to be done."

Fabian and Father Josef stood together staring over the sea for several moments without speaking. Fabian turned to Father Josef, and with a smile he said, "Thank you, Father. Your words give me peace. Good night, Father." He then went to his tent.

Father Josef stood facing the dark and shining sea. In time his thoughts turned to the orphanage; how could he help those unfortunate children? Father Josef looked up into the sky and prayed to God for guidance.

The next morning Peter was up at daybreak. He went from tent to tent stirring the soldiers and instructing them to assemble on the beach in an hour. Peter and the men had been in Pahlavi for three weeks. A supply tent had been set up to store all the supplies they had collected. For the past several days, Peter had made an inventory of the supplies. He believed they had enough to reach Africa.

The men gathered in a large, open area just outside their tent city. The Iranian army had given the soldiers supplies in large wooden crates (boxes). The crates now lay empty on the beach. Peter stood on one of the crates so he could see among the soldiers. Peter said, "It is time to assemble all of our supplies and prepare to move across the desert. We will begin our journey an hour before sunup tomorrow. Divide into the teams you were in during our march across the Caucasus Mountains. Aleksy will be our quartermaster (a quartermaster is responsible for distributing supplies) Fabian, Dominik and Henryk will assist Aleksy. Every team should come by the supply tent and be issued their supplies before the sun goes down today." When Peter had finished, he dismissed the men and began making final preparations for their journey to Africa.

The news of the impending departure had taken Father Josef and the other men by surprise, but it was time they should leave. The people of Pahlavi and the Iranian army had been very good to the soldiers. It was best they not overstay their welcome.

When the soldiers were dismissed, Father Josef left the encampment and returned to the orphanage. The sisters greeted him warmly. Sister Catherine said, "Father, how good to see you. We did not expect your return to be so soon."

Father Josef said, "Preparations are being made to leave for Africa tomorrow. I wanted to say goodbye and visit the children before I left." Sister Catherine said, "I will take you to Mother Superior. She will be happy to see you again." Father Josef followed Sister Catherine as she moved across the grounds of the orphanage into the building where they found Mother Superior Mary Teresa sitting at her desk.

When Father Josef entered the room, she was surprised, but her face instantly turned into a warm smile. Mother Superior said, "Father Josef, it is wonderful to see you again. Please come and sit down." She motioned to a chair that was sitting in front of her desk. Sister Catherine excused herself and left the room. Father Josef and Mother Superior talked about the children and how best to prepare them for the time when they would leave the orphanage. Father Josef shared ideas that he thought would help the sisters with the children's education.

After some time discussing these things, he said, "There were two reasons for my visit today. First, I came to share my thoughts with you about the orphanage; the second reason I came was because tomorrow we leave for Africa. I will think of the sisters in Pahlavi and the children often." Father Josef then rose from his chair and said, "I would like to say goodbye to the children. Will you take me to them?"

Mother Superior said, "Of course, Father, but first I would like to show you something. Please come this way." Father Josef followed Mother Superior to a room on the second floor. It was not a large room. It had just enough room for a bed, a small desk, a chair, and a small table. On top of the table was a candle, a Bible, paper for writing, a quill and a small bottle of ink. A quill is a bird's wing feather that is used for writing. Father Josef was confused and turned to look at Mother Superior. She said, "Maybe God has a place for you here." Father Josef had not considered this. Was it God's calling that he should stay and help the children at the orphanage? The room had a window which overlooked the children's playgrounds.

Father Josef walked to the window and looked at the grounds below. From here he was able to see the activities of the orphanage. The sisters each had their own small group of children. Each group had a game they were playing. He loved hearing the children's voices so full of excitement. For a moment his thoughts went back to his school in Bavaria. He turned to speak to Mother Superior but discovered he was alone in the room. He again turned to the window to watch the children below. After several moments, he left the room and walked downstairs where he found Mother Superior waiting for him.

She said nothing as he approached. Father Josef said, "I must leave now to help the soldiers prepare for the journey to Africa. Thank you for everything you have shared with me."

Mother Superior said, "God be with you, Father."

Father Josef said, "God be with you as well." With that he left the orphanage and returned to the soldiers' encampment.

The next morning, it was still dark when the soldiers began to assemble into formation. A formation is a column of soldiers who march together in files. A file is between eight and sixteen men. Peter was walking among the men checking to see if the final preparations for the journey had been completed. When everything was in order, he returned to the front of the formation to find Father Josef waiting for him. Peter said, "Father, will you be marching with me at the head of the formation?"

Father Josef said, "Peter, I have decided to return to the orphanage. The children have a greater need of me than the soldiers. I must say goodbye to you and the men. I will always remember you as my friends and brothers."

Peter said, "Have you told the men about your decision to stay in Pahlavi?"

Father Josef said, "No, it was only this morning that I decided to stay. I did not wish to delay your departure by saying long goodbyes to the men. Please let them know they will be in my heart and prayers always. Goodbye, my son." With that said, Father Josef and Peter hugged each other in a strong embrace of true affection. Father Josef then left for the orphanage, and Peter readied his men for the journey across the desert to Africa.

The men were ready both mentally and physically for the journey ahead. They had done their best to prepare for every imaginable event. However, for all their planning, our soldiers could never have guessed what would happen next.

It is said that big surprises sometimes come in small packages. This is indeed true, my dear readers. Read on, and you shall see what I mean.

CHAPTER VI
The Soldiers Find a Sack Full of Mischief

The soldiers had been marching across the Iranian desert for several days. They had made it through the freezing cold of Siberia, and now they would have to endure the burning heat of the desert. But let us not forget, my dear readers, our soldiers are determined and resourceful men.

Navigation through the desert is difficult. The sand dunes change because of the desert wind, and there are few landmarks to use as guides, so instead the soldiers used signs from the sky to find their way. At night there is a star that has been used for navigation for centuries. It is called the North Star or the Polaris Star. The star lies nearly in a direct line with the earth's axis. The earth's axis is an invisible line drawn through the center of the earth from the North Pole to the South Pole around which the earth spins. Because the Polaris star is in the sky above the North Pole, the soldier can always use it as a point of reference. When the Polaris star is directly in front of him, he knows he is traveling north and when directly behind him, he knows he is traveling south. If Polaris is on his right, he is traveling west, and if it is on his left, he is traveling east. Peter was told by the Iranian army to travel in a south-west direction across the desert in order to reach Africa. The soldiers were careful to make sure the star was always behind them and to the right.

The soldiers knew an average man could walk a mile in twenty minutes, but walking in the sand was slow work. They were carrying supplies and walking in the blazing heat, often climbing uphill or down with sand slipping out from under their feet. Because of the conditions, they knew that they were likely walking less than average. They estimated they could walk two miles per hour. But how do you think they could tell when an hour had passed? Our soldiers had not picked up a watch in their travels because the people of the desert had no need for such things. They could estimate what time it was by the position of the sun in the sky and the length of their shadows. They could also continue to check if the direction they were walking was correct by making sure their shadows fell to the right in morning and to the left in the late afternoon.

When the sun first rose over the horizon, the soldiers' shadows were very long. As the day progressed, their shadows grew shorter and shorter. When their shadows were short but not completely beneath their feet, they knew that it was time to pitch their tents again and settle in for a long rest while waiting for the hot sun to pass over them. They would walk, watching the position of their shadows, heading southwest as instructed until sometime after the sun had completely fallen behind the horizon in the west.

Day after day our soldiers carefully rationed their food and water. Walking from sunup until their shadows were short and then again walking in the late afternoon until the sun had completely set, they slowly made their way across the desert. The soldiers knew the sun was in the sky about sixteen hours per day, and they were resting about four of those hours. That meant they were walking for twelve hours per day. If they kept a pace of about two miles per hour, they would have ample rations to reach their destination, only needing to find additional water twice during their journey.

While the soldiers were resting and the sun was high in the sky, they noticed a strange sight in the distance. They could barely make out a small figure traveling toward them. As it came closer, the soldiers could see it was a young boy carrying a sack over his shoulder. It was a curious scene, and the soldiers watched with interest as he approached. After a short while, Peter and Dominik moved forward to meet the boy.

Before long, Peter, Dominik and the boy were facing each other. During the three weeks Peter had spent in Pahlavi, he had learned to understand a few words in the Arabic language. He said, "As Salam Alaykom." This means "peace be upon you" in Arabic. This is how people in Arabic countries greet each other. The young boy looked at Peter and the soldiers with great interest. He did not speak. On his shoulder the boy was carrying a sack which he placed on the ground at his feet. The young boy was our friend, Amin.

It was totally by chance that Amin had come upon the soldiers. But I wonder, my dear readers, if there really is this thing called "chance." Perhaps it was providence. Providence is described as divine guidance. Peter had a goatskin container of water attached with a leather strap around his neck. He took the water container and offered Amin a drink. Amin took the water and drank several long gulps until he felt totally satisfied. He handed the goatskin container back to Peter. Peter and Dominik were curious about the boy and concerned about his well-being. They wondered if he was lost or if he was a member of a nearby tribe of nomads.

Amin had been walking in the desert for many hours. As you may remember, dear readers, his father had instructed him to return home before dark. Amin wanted to obey his father, but it was just impossible for him to leave Cubby in the desert without any chance of survival. Perhaps the soldiers would help save his bear.

Amin picked up the sack he had placed next to his feet. With both hands, he extended the sack to Peter. Peter thought the boy was giving him the sack in exchange for the water. Peter took the sack, not intending to keep it but thought it was a good opportunity to see what was inside. When Peter looked inside the sack, he was totally taken by surprise. Inside the sack was a small bear curled up in a ball fast asleep. Peter turned to Dominik and said, "Look at this. Can you believe your eyes?" Dominik looked in the sack and began to laugh hysterically. By this time the other soldiers had gathered around Peter, Dominik and Amin. They were very curious to see what was in the sack. Dominik lifted Cubby out of the sack and held him close to his chest. Cubby placed both paws on Dominik's shoulders and looked around from one soldier to another. No one expected to find a bear in the sack.

Amin pointed to Cubby and then to Peter in a gesture to ask Peter if he wanted Cubby as his bear. Peter turned to Dominik and said, "I think he is asking me if I want the bear."

Dominik said, "Let's keep him. He can be our mascot." A mascot is an animal adopted by a group as its symbol and is supposed to bring good luck. The furry bundle reminded Fabian of a time when he was a boy on a farm. He said, "I had a dog on my family's farm. It was a wonderful pet. Our dog became a part of our family."

Aleksy said, "Fabian, you have been getting too much sun. This is a bear not a dog. Did your family have pet bears on your farm?"

Fabian said, "What's the difference? A pet is a pet. We can take care of him."

With that Aleksy exclaimed, "Who knows how to take care of a bear?"

Dominik said, "Ok, ok, so the bear is not a dog, and no one has ever taken care of a bear. But if we keep him, I will do my part to help take care of him." Then he turned to Peter and said, "Peter, what about you? Do you want to keep the little guy?"

Peter turned to the men and said, "Men, we all have to agree. The bear will be taking part of our water and food that we need to get to Africa. I don't think it will take much to feed him, but we must remember we do not have much to spare. So I will leave it up to a vote. Everyone in agreement to keep the bear say 'tak' (tak pronounced tualk) or 'nie' (nie pronounced nyeh)." The soldiers gave such a resounding "TAK!" It sounded like a group of Vikings screaming into

ONCE A HERO

battle. Their approval could not have been misunderstood. There was no need to ask who among them would say "nie."

Peter turned to Amin, smiled, and shook his head up and down to mean they would take the bear. From the soldiers' loud response, Amin was thinking maybe this could be an opportunity. If the soldiers wanted his bear, perhaps they would pay something in return. Trading in the Middle East is how business is done. Amin held out his hand.

Peter turned to Dominik and said, "I think he would like something in return. Do you have any ideas what to give him?"

Fabian said, "I will give him my knife."

Aleksy said, "I will give him some of my food ration."

Dominik said, "I have some coins an Iranian soldier gave me. I will give them to him as well." Peter collected the knife, a can of corned beef, and some coins and offered them to Amin. Amin looked at what the soldiers had offered and a huge smile came across his face. He collected his bounty and shook his head up and down in agreement. Amin turned to head home excited to show his father what a wonderful trade he had made. As he turned to go Peter said, "Wait."

Amin stopped and turned back to face Peter. Peter retrieved a goat skin container of water and handed it to Amin. He was concerned about the young boy, not knowing how far he would have to travel without water. Amin took the water and said, "Shukran" which means "thank you" in the Arabic language. He then turned and began walking back in the direction from which he had come. The soldiers watched until Amin disappeared over the horizon.

Now all of the soldiers' attention was focused on their new little bear.

"What is our bear's name?" Fabian asked.

"Let's name him Wojtek" (pronounced Voy-check) which means "smiling warrior" in Polish," suggested Dominik.

Peter said, "That sounds like a good name. Let's put it to a vote. Everybody listen up. All in favor of naming our bear Wojtek say 'tak,' all opposed say 'nie.' The soldiers made such a sound when they responded with "TAK!" camels ten miles away must have looked up and wondered, "What was that?"

"Wojtek it is," said Peter.

The soldiers were very happy. The little bear was more than a mascot; Wojtek put laughter in the soldier's hearts and lifted their spirits. They were now more than ever determined to finish a mission that some had thought impossible.

So, my dear readers, for a small knife, a can of corned beef and a few Iranian coins, Cubby had found a new home. The soldiers named him Wojtek: A big name for such a small bear. But as you shall see, it would prove to be a very fitting name for a bear that would one day show courage in the face of certain death.

CHAPTER VII
Wojtek Arrives in Africa

During the first night in the desert, the soldiers tried to feed Wojtek corned beef, fish jerky, and a number of other things, but he would eat none of them. After a while, Fabian realized that Wojtek was so young that he probably could not eat anything but liquids. The soldiers had a couple of goats the people of Iran had given them. Fabian had the idea to feed their little bear goat's milk—great idea but how?

Well, soldiers are creative and can find solutions to most problems. They got a goatskin container and made a sort of nipple on the end. From this their little bear drank and drank and drank until all the milk was gone. During the whole feeding process, Wojtek was humming like a well-tuned engine in a European sports car.

Now that their little friend was well-fed, he curled up in a ball and went to sleep. The soldiers did not want to put Wojtek in the sand or place him back in his bag, so Dominik said, "I will let the little guy sleep with me." Before long night time came, and the calm of the desert night found all of the soldiers sleeping soundly. Wojtek was curled up next to Dominik on a blanket inside a small tent with two other soldiers. All was going well.

An hour before sunrise the desert came alive with a bloodcurdling scream. The scream was coming from Dominik's tent. Everyone jumped to their feet. In an instant, the soldiers were up and out of their tents. Expecting the worst, they armed with whatever weapons they could find. Peter found Dominik standing outside his tent wearing only his pants. Most of the soldiers slept without their shirt or shoes. With a crazed look on his face, Dominik was standing there staring across the desert with his mouth open. One would think that he had just seen a ghost. Peter said, "Dominik, what is wrong?" As Peter spoke, he noticed that Dominik's chest was blood red, and there were small impressions that looked like teeth marks. Dominik said, "The bear was sleeping next to me, and when I woke, he had half of my chest in his mouth." Oh, my dear readers, Wojtek was still a little baby. He was only doing what came naturally. Dominik was too much in a state of shock to continue with any further explanations. So let me tell you what happened.

Wojtek curled up next to Dominik with his head on Dominik's chest. To little Wojtek it was the same as his mother's chest where he got milk. So when he woke up the next morning, he was hungry. Wojtek attached his mouth to Dominik's chest, and with all the force of a hydraulic pump, he attempted to get breakfast. Dominik awoke from a sound sleep. His eyes flashed open, his hair stood straight up, and his mouth opened wide without a sound coming out. He was in sheer pain and terror. All of a sudden with his lungs filled with air, Dominik let out a scream that stormed like a hurricane through every tent in the camp. He did not know if he was being eaten alive or going through the worst nightmare of his life. He jumped to his feet and ran outside the tent in a state of shock. This is where Peter found him. The scream that Dominik made had frightened the two soldiers that shared his tent so badly they were in as much shock as Dominik.

Eerie silence overtook the entire camp as the soldiers stood with weapons in hand trying to determine what was happening. The desert looked empty. What was going on?

As Peter, Dominik and the two other men stood staring from one to another, a rustling noise from inside the tent got their attention. They turned to look and saw little Wojtek walking out of the tent wondering what all the fuss was about. But more importantly, he was wondering where was breakfast?

This was the first night Wojtek spent with the soldiers. Things got off to a rocky start, but with every new day, the soldiers learned a little better how to take care of their little bear.

ONCE A HERO

Wojtek was tiny enough to sleep anywhere, but he preferred to snuggle with the soldiers in their beds, much as he would have slept with his mother in the wild. Dominik's experience had taught the soldiers a lesson—wear shirts when sleeping with Wojtek.

The care and attention the soldiers gave to their little bear, combined with being bottle-fed until he was old enough to eat solid food, caused Wojtek to bond with the soldiers as if they were his mother. The soldiers became his family. Happy and carefree, Wojtek would walk beside the soldiers when they marched through the desert. Sometimes he would accidently trip them and make a soldier fall when he ran between his legs like he used to do with his mother. When someone got tripped because of Wojtek's antics (clowning around), it always made the soldiers laugh. To Wojtek they were all on a fun journey. Playing in the sand and causing all the unintended mischief just made the journey that much more fun.

The soldiers showed great skill navigating the desert. They arrived at the British Command in the exact number of days which they had planned. Peter and the men had done an excellent job during every facet of their journey.

CHAPTER VIII

The Soldiers Join the British

The British Command was officially known as the 8th Army. They were being assembled to fight a brilliant German general known as Wustenfuchs which is German for the Desert Fox. The Desert Fox's real name was Erwin Rommel. He had conquered most of North Africa and appeared to be unstoppable.

Erwin Rommel was the second of four children. Erwin was small in stature but was known to be physically strong. His father was a professor. Young Erwin's father decided that he should make a career in the army. Erwin made below average grades, so a profession that required higher academics was out of the question. To Erwin's father, the army was the only answer, but Erwin did not agree; he wanted to be an engineer. Unfortunately for Erwin and the rest of the world, World War II started, and young Erwin was left with little choice but to join the German army.

Erwin Rommel proved to be a brave and cunning soldier. He was highly decorated with medals and soon became an officer in the German infantry. Hitler was so impressed with Rommel's leadership abilities that he promoted him to Field Marshal of North Africa. Rommel took command of the 7th Armor Panzer Division. This was an elite armored division (tanks) that General Rommel would make legendary as a result of their many military victories in spite of being outnumbered two or three to one in every battle. The Desert Fox defeated the French army in seven major battles. The American army was occupied fighting the Nazis in Europe. The British Command was the last hope of stopping Rommel.

The British Command needed men for their newly formed army.

When the Polish soldiers appeared out of nowhere from the Iranian Desert, the British were pleasantly surprised to find a trained artillery unit at their disposal. However these brave soldiers were in much disrepair. Their journey had taken them from the Russian gulags, through the freezing terrain of Siberia, over the Caspian Sea, and across the Iranian Desert. The men looked like flesh stretched across skeletons. Their clothes were ragged and torn, and those who had shoes had little more than rags tied around their feet. Their hair and beards were long and matted in dirt. The soldiers' appearances revealed the unique hell of warfare.

The British were sympathetic with the plight of these courageous men. Rather than separate them, they gave these Polish warriors their own place in the British 22nd Artillery Supply Command. They became the 22nd Artillery Supply Command, Polish II Corps.

Over the next several weeks, the soldiers were given supplies and helped to build a mess hall and barracks. A mess hall is a place where soldiers cook and eat their food. A barracks is a building that houses beds and wall lockers (individual stand-alone closets). They also constructed a 500-gallon water tank and modified it to provide not only drinking water but also showers. Next the soldiers built a clubhouse where they enjoyed leisure time. Some of the furniture for the clubhouse was brought in by the British supply lines, and some pieces the soldiers built using wood from shipping crates. The British furnished the soldiers with a phonograph (record player) and a few records. But what was a phonograph without electricity? The British took care of the electricity problem with newly invented generators. They had music, lights, food, water and showers. Yes, my dear readers, the soldiers were living in a fashion that they had not known for a long time.

And what of Wojtek while all this was going on? Well, you can imagine the British soldiers had been quite surprised when they discovered the rugged and worn soldiers from Poland were carrying a baby bear with them! Right from the start, Wojtek was a celebrity.

Soldiers from nearby units heard of the baby bear the Polish unit was housing and couldn't wait to visit. With each visit from neighboring soldiers came a little treat. Men brought honey, meat, fruits, bread, marmalade and anything else they could get their hands on to feed him. Wojtek thrived on both the healthy diet and the attention. It was no time at all before Wojtek grew from a small cub, weighing 1 stone (about 10 pounds) at the time when our friend Amin gave him to the soldiers, into a bear that weighed more than 43 stone (600 pounds) and stood over six feet tall. He was a sight to see indeed.

From the day he first arrived in the camp and every day thereafter, Wojtek watched the soldiers just as he had watched his mother. He learned to stand on his hind legs and walk upright just like the soldiers. When the soldiers would march, Wojtek rushed over and marched with them. When a soldier saluted him, Wojtek would salute back. Wojtek was becoming a soldier's soldier.

Wojtek loved to wrestle. From the time he had been a small cub, the soldiers had wrestled with him. At first, when he was small, he would wrestle the soldiers one-on-one. As he grew, groups of soldiers would wrestle Wojtek all at one time. Even though this may sound like they were ganging up on poor Wojtek, the soldiers needed all the help they could get. Sometimes he would catch a soldier and carry him under his arm while he continued to wrestle the remaining soldiers with the other arm. Wojtek was his own one-bear football team, and one of the soldiers would often become his ball. This genial (cheerful) giant was always just playing and never intended to hurt anyone. But when playing with a 600-pound bear, one should expect to get a few bumps and bruises. The soldiers always took their aches and pains in good spirits. After all, there was nothing like wrestling a giant bear to get your mind off of the hardships of war.

Whenever the soldiers would travel to military camps to make munitions deliveries, Wojtek would always ride with Peter in the lead truck. He would sit in the passenger seat with his big arm hanging out the window and his huge head almost touching the roof of the truck. When Wojtek rode through the village, people turned and stared in disbelief. Some stood with their eyes as big as saucers and their mouths open, unable to speak. Others would stare up into heaven, shake their heads, and pray they were seeing an illusion. If it was not an illusion, there could be only one other explanation—they were losing their minds.

Wojtek liked to raid the mess hall when nobody was looking. The doors to the mess hall were never locked, and Wojtek could open a door as well as any soldier. After being prevented from entering the mess hall alone on a number of occasions, he learned to wait until the soldiers were busy with other duties. When no one was looking, he would casually stroll into the mess hall and help himself to anything that was not under lock and key. Wojtek found eating alone to be a most satisfactory way of dining.

Wojtek became very proficient at working the showers in the bath hut. On one occasion, when he was all alone, he took a five-hundred-gallon shower. As a result of Wojtek's leisurely bath, the soldiers had to go without water for two days until their water could be resupplied by the British. After that little episode, any time Wojtek was noticed hanging around the shower hut, this precocious (unusually advanced) bear got everyone's attention. But it is said, "There is some good in all things." We shall see how Wojtek's love for a relaxing shower actually saved many of the soldiers' lives.

The Germans recruited nomads in Iraq to infiltrate the British Command's military camps. The Iraqis would conduct surprise attacks on the British camps, and many soldiers were killed as a result of these raids. Food, equipment and many other valuable supplies were carried off by the bandits. Anything the bandits could not carry, they destroyed.

One night when the soldiers were preparing to turn in for the night, an Iraqi was able to sneak past the guards on duty and make his way into camp. His mission was to get any information he could concerning the camp, including the number of soldiers, the location of the soldiers' weapons, and the time when the camp would be most vulnerable to attack. Iraqi bandits were waiting outside the camp preparing to attack. They needed the spy's information before attacking, so they could catch the soldiers unaware and disable them before they could get to their weapons. Once inside, the Iraqi decided to hide in the bath hut until everyone was sound asleep. This proved to be a very unwise choice for a hiding place.

It just so happened that about this time, Wojtek decided it would be nice to take a bath. The camp was quiet and dark, so there was little chance of him being disturbed. Upon entering the hut, Wojtek's keen sense of smell detected something different in the air. It was dark, but the hut had an open roof, and there was plenty of moonlight. He noticed what looked like a shadow in the corner of the hut. Wojtek stood on his hind legs, stretching his gigantic body to almost the top of the hut, and began walking in the direction of the shadow. Suddenly when Wojtek realized this was not one of the soldiers, he began to get very angry just as his mother would have done if she felt her cub was in danger. Wojtek flung his huge arms back and forth and let out a tempestuous (violent) roar that caused the mountains to tremble. The terrified Iraqi began to scream in horror. The man had nowhere to run. Wojtek had him cornered. He began beating his chest while at the same time growling and showing his massive teeth. His dinner-plate sized paws with six-inch claws were cutting back and forth in the air. The spy was in a state of unadulterated (pure) horror. By now the entire camp was up with weapons in hand rushing toward the shower hut. Terrified of being eaten, the man remained in the corner of the shower hut screaming at the top of his voice. Once the soldiers arrived and took the spy into custody, Wojtek dropped to all four legs and amiably walked out of the hut.

The soldiers took the Iraqi to a hut for questioning. This was all very curious to Wojtek, so he followed the group. The soldiers radioed British Command and informed them of their situation. An interpreter was requested. Once the interpreter arrived, the questioning began.

At first the spy refused to say anything. He sat there in sullen defiance. A soldier standing guard inside the hut noticed that Wojtek was standing just outside the door. He decided it would be a good idea to give their defiant spy a little peek at who was waiting on the other side of the door. The soldier opened the door of the hut. Wojtek stuck his mammoth-sized head inside to observe the situation. The spy looked in the direction of the open door, and his unyielding attitude suddenly changed. His brow wrinkled into a question mark. His face began to distort in panic. The spy became delirious, and his babble was incoherent. The soldier closed the door to the hut. Now the spy would talk. In fact he talked so much the soldiers couldn't write it down fast enough. He went on for the next half hour giving them detailed information about the planned raid. Soon he had confessed all, and the soldiers immediately radioed British Command with all the details. The raid was foiled, and more than 100 of the enemy were captured within the hour. Wojtek had saved the day. He was the soldiers' hero.

Like many humans who have served in the armed forces, Wojtek developed a taste for beer. Beer was a common drink in Africa because a lot of the water in the desert was contaminated (poison). Making beer was a way of life in many parts of Africa. The village people often drank beer to get the water they needed without the fear of getting sick or maybe dying from contaminated water. The soldiers enjoyed the locally brewed beer and kept a small supply in the mess hall food pantry. When they were relaxing and having a beer, the soldiers would share one with their buddy Wojtek. Except for his huge head, massive teeth, six-inch claws and fur coat, Wojtek was just one of the boys.

Wojtek was also fascinated by the sight of the soldiers smoking cigarettes. After a while, when he saw a soldier light up a cigarette, he would walk over to him and stick out his huge paw to bum a cigarette.

The cigarette had to be lit or Wojtek would throw it on the ground. After he had a lit cigarette, he would stick it in his mouth for a while and then swallow it whole, letting out a puff of smoke. Wojtek's ludicrous (ridiculous) cigarette smoking always made the soldiers laugh. However, one day it was not so funny; it nearly scared a brave man to death.

It was a well known fact that there was going to be a new commanding officer for the North African British Command. A change of command took place about every eighteen months. What the soldiers didn't know was he had already arrived. The man was a British army colonel with a distinguished military record.

The colonel walked smartly with an air of authority. In addition to an immaculate uniform that did not reveal the slightest hint of a wrinkle, he wore highly polished knee-high boots and sported a finely trimmed mustache. He had a nervous and excitable temperament. The colonel expected everything to be in its place in tip-top military fashion. His reputation as a crack (slang for excellent) military commander preceded him wherever he went. He was a veteran of many war campaigns and was known to be a brave soldier.

During war time, the change of command formalities were ignored. As a result, the new commander had assumed his post unnoticed by most of the troops. The lack of attention had worked to the colonel's advantage. It was his intention to make unannounced visits to the troops' compounds (camps). He wanted to observe firsthand the unrehearsed day-to-day life of a British soldier serving in the desert.

Included in his agenda was a visit to the Polish soldiers' compound. The colonel had heard stories of how the Polish soldiers had survived a trek from Siberia to Africa but was not impressed. He was of the opinion that these men were being overly embraced. The colonel had remarked to his adjutant officers that surely some of the stories about the Polish soldiers were exaggerated. An adjutant officer is someone who assists the commanding officer in carrying out orders.

The colonel decided to see for himself how these men compared to the British soldiers. He paid his visit to the Polish soldiers' camp. His doubts about the soldiers' credibility vanished as a result of a remarkable chance encounter.

A British military uniform was a common sight among the Polish soldiers, so they paid little attention to the colonel as he walked around from one hut to another. Aleksy had been up since daybreak organizing munitions shipments. It was getting close to noon and time for chow (lunch). Before eating he decided to take a break outside the hut and have a cigarette and beer. Aleksy proceeded to get himself a beer and light up a smoke. His actions caught the watchful eye of Wojtek who was sitting under a large canopy. He ran over to Aleksy and stuck out a huge paw. Aleksy laughed, went inside, and got Wojtek a beer. He then lit a cigarette and placed it between Wojtek's claws. Now all was well. What could be more natural than a man and his animal companion standing outside a hut having a beer and a cigarette while taking a well-deserved break?

Suddenly out of nowhere, the colonel turned the corner and came face to face with Wojtek. He stood frozen, staring into Wojtek's fierce-looking face. Wojtek stared back at the colonel while casually flipping the lit cigarette into his mouth and slowly eating it. The look on the colonel's face confessed that his brain did not believe what his eyes were seeing. Wojtek moved his head a little closer to the colonel and let out a puff of smoke. The colonel staggered backwards. Aleksy was caught off guard by the whole spectacle but immediately jumped into action. He dropped his beer and grabbed the colonel by the shirt to prevent him from falling. The poor man was almost in a dead faint.

Wojtek, sensing he might be in trouble, dropped to all four feet and ran back under the canopy. There he sat with his big front paws interlocked across his chest looking everywhere except in the direction of Aleksy. Wojtek was the perfect picture of innocence.

Aleksy had never seen this man before, but he noticed the colonel insignia on the lapel of his shirt. He thought to himself, "The commanding officer is always a colonel. No, couldn't be. Have mercy, Mother Mary, he must be." Wojtek had just informally met the new commanding officer of the British North African Command.

After returning to British Command Headquarters, the colonel was still attempting to recover from his trip to the Polish compound. In his office with a shaky hand holding a glass of brandy, he commented to a member of his staff, "Lieutenant Blair, I underestimated those Polish chaps. Anyone who can carry on the duties of war and sleep at night without having the least concern for a 600-pound beast roaming the camp is man enough in my book. Yes, Blair, I will state unequivocally that those are some of the bravest soldiers I have ever set my eyes upon."

CHAPTER IX
Where is Private Wojtek Bear?

During a war, tens of thousands of pounds of supplies, munitions, equipment and soldiers need to be moved to strategic locations for the purpose of conducting battles and occupying conquered territory. This transport system is called the "supply lines." You can imagine the army with the shortest and most efficient supply lines would have a compelling advantage. Consequently, a good deal of effort is spent seeding and developing the best routes.

Moving freight over water is a far more efficient means of transport than moving it over land. In addition, the route from Europe to Africa by land is much longer than by water, and this would require the traversing of caravans through hundreds of miles of enemy territory. Both the Germans and the British were keen to transport their goods over the shorter water route.

The Mediterranean Sea is bordered by several European countries on the north and by the continent of Africa on its south side. Its significance in the history of the region cannot be overstated. During WWII, the army controlling this body of water, and consequently the most direct supply line, would have a distinct advantage.

At the time, Germany's naval fleet, the Kriegsmarine, was unmatched. Their presence in the Mediterranean was menacing. In addition, the formidable Luftwaffe (German air force) was providing cover from the sky. Between these naval and air forces, the Germans were very successful in battling the Royal British Air Force and bombing British military compounds. As a result, the British Royal Navy suffered heavy losses in the battles against the Germans in the Mediterranean Sea. Soon, Rommel was in control of the entire Mediterranean

African coast allowing fuel for the 7th Panzer Division, ammunition for their guns, and food for the troops to be quickly and efficiently delivered effectively giving the Axis countries a major tactical advantage during WWII.

While England and Germany were battling over territory in Africa, more and more countries were being roped into war. Germany had conquered Austria, Poland, Belgium, the Netherlands and Romania. Additionally, they had made alliances with Italy, Japan and the Soviet Union though soon they would turn on the Soviet Union. This coalition was known as the "Axis" powers. At the same time, Britain had formed alliances with France and China forming the union known as the "Allied Powers."

Though Rommel was successful in commandeering control of the Mediterranean and the 7th Panzer Division was winning battle after battle on the ground, the tide was about to turn. Two events changed Rommel's destiny: the Japanese bombed Hawaii, an American territory, and Hitler attacked Russia. These two events caused the powerful United States to be called to arms and the Soviet Union to switch sides, leaving the Axis powers and joining the Allies.

After the infamous Japanese attack on Pearl Harbor, located on the island of Oahu in Hawaii, the United States quickly prepared for war. The U.S. sent naval support to the Mediterranean to aid the British in their battles against the German Kriegsmarine. With the decisive help of the mighty forces of the American navy, the Allies gained control over the Mediterranean. Rommel was now forced to bring supplies across the unforgiving desert.

Rommel's supply line advantage was now terminated. Without control in the Mediterranean Sea, his new means of transport by land was slow and susceptible to being destroyed by sandstorms or bombings raids by the Royal British Air Force. The American elite fighter squadrons also wreaked havoc on Rommel's forces. They were responsible for preventing thousands of gallons of fuel from reaching their destination. Before long, Rommel's 7th Panzer Tank Division was running critically low on fuel. His soldiers were almost without food and other much needed supplies.

Rommel's problems became even greater after Hitler attacked Russia in what was to be the largest invasion in the history of warfare. The Germans called this "Operation Barbarossa." Barbarossa means red beard in Italian. Four million Italian and German soldiers invaded the Russian borders and within days, they had penetrated 300 miles deep into the Soviet Union.

Already crippled by the Allied invasion in the Mediterranean, Rommel was dealt another blow by his own Fuhrer. Hitler ordered the Afrika Corp's Luftwaffe to return from Africa and join Operation Barbarossa. This left Rommel without air support. Next, the newest member of the Allies sent ground troops (infantry) and artillery into Africa to support the British 8th Army in ground combat. The American's tour de force (impressive performance) alongside the British 8th Army proved to be the final blow against Rommel. Without the help of the Luftwaffe, he was stranded. There was no victory possible and no escape. Over 100,000 German soldiers were taken prisoners of war, and the Allies were victorious in Africa.

Rommel was secretly flown out of Africa to Hitler's headquarters in Berlin, Germany to answer for his defeat. He was demoted and reassigned to northern France. Rommel felt betrayed. He no longer believed in the German leadership's position on the war. Rommel did not feel it possible for the Axis Powers to win the war. He was still a patriot of Germany but not of the Nazi regime. A patriot is someone who loves his country and is willing to risk his life to defend it.

Rommel looked forward to the time when the war was over, and he would be re-united with his wife and children. But he was never to see the end of the war. It was Rommel's destiny to meet with an untimely death. He was accused by the Gestapo (German secret police) of being involved in a plot to assassinate Adolf Hitler. As a result of the accusation, Rommel was given two alternatives: his wife and children could go to prison while he would be forced to continue to serve the Nazis or he could take cyanide (deadly poison) tablets. Rommel took the cyanide.

Rommel was a hero to the German people, and he was respected by his enemies. Prisoners of war captured by Rommel's troops were always treated humanely. He even refused orders from Nazi headquarters to execute prisoners that had been captured in battle. To avoid a backlash by the German people the Nazis said that Rommel had died because of a heart attack. Now, my dear readers, you know the truth about General Rommel's sad death.

Africa and the Mediterranean were now in the hands of the Allies. The 22nd Artillery Supply Company and the Polish II Corps received orders to go to Italy. They were to support the front-line troops battling their way to Rome. Peter, Aleksy, Fabian, Dominik, Henryk and the other soldiers who made up Polish II Corps found themselves in the port of Alexandria, Egypt. They were waiting to board a ship headed to Naples, Italy, where they would join the Allies.

The port officials in Alexandria refused to allow Wojtek to board the ship. Only soldiers could make the journey. Wild animals and mascots were prohibited. To the soldiers, Wojtek was certainly not a wild animal, and he was more than a mascot. He was their comrade. Wojtek had been a source of joy during the heartaches of separation from their families and the grueling battles in Africa. Wojtek was a hero that had saved their lives. The soldiers were determined not to leave Wojtek behind. In absolute dire straits and determined not to leave Wojtek behind, the soldiers called upon an old friend to see what help he could offer.

During the solders' two years in Africa they had remained in contact with Father Josef back in Iran. Father Josef still considered himself a chaplain in the Polish army. In addition to his duties at the orphanage he had aided many a wayward soldier that had come through Iran in his efforts to join the Allies. The soldiers had kept Father Josef informed of all the major events that had happened since their separation. He was aware of Wojtek and his intimate relationship with his comrades. The soldiers radioed Father Josef an urgent appeal to help them to keep Wojtek from being separated from their group. I should point out, my dear readers, that a chaplain does not command troops and give orders. But a request made by a respected chaplain carries much influence in the military.

Father Josef sent a request via the Iranian army to the military office in Cairo. His message was relayed as follows: "I am Father Josef, a chaplain in the Polish army. A new Polish soldier wishing to join the Polish II Corps has arrived in Cairo. It is my recommendation that his request be granted. He will contribute greatly to the Allied forces. His name is Wojtek Bear. He is known and revered as brave and steadfast (direct in purpose) among the soldiers serving in the Polish II Corps." Father Josef's request was granted.

The newest member of the Polish II Corps was Wojtek Bear. He was given a service number, the rank of private and a pay book. The port officials in Alexandria were astounded but had no choice but to allow Private Wojtek Bear to board the ship.

Once the ship arrived in Naples, a British officer by the name of Captain Archibald Brown was in port to help process soldiers that had just arrived from Alexandria, Egypt. Among his everyday duties was checking the crew manifest and speaking with the freshly arrived soldiers. But this would be no typical day for Captain Brown.

Brown had already spoken with every single member of the 22nd Artillery Supply Company of Polish II Corp...except one. After looking at his roster there was only one soldier, Private Wojtek Bear, who was not accounted for. The documents showed that Private Wojtek belonged to the unit. He had a service number and a pay book, but the soldier himself seemed to have vanished without a trace.

The soldiers were assembled in the port waiting for further instructions. Brown walked in front of the group and called out the missing soldier's name, but there was no response. He called out his name for the second and third time but still no response. Brown was now in an agitated state and asked in a loud and demanding voice, "Why is Private Wojtek not coming forward?"

Dominik stepped forward and responded, "Sir, I am sure Private Wojtek would be happy to comply with your request, but he only understands Polish and a wee bit of Persian."

Brown said, "Well, soldier, since you do speak the King's English and Polish, lead me to him so I can confirm his arrival." Captain Brown was then led to the rear of the unit where sat a full-grown Syrian bear with his arms crossed upon his chest. His head was held high and was sniffing the sea air while taking in all the interesting sights going on in the port. Dominik said, "Sir, may I introduce Private Wojtek Bear?"

CHAPTER X

The Battle of Monte Cassion

It was January 1944 when our friends, the Polish soldiers, arrived in Italia (Italy in English). The Allied forces were on the move and hellbent to conquer Rome. As members of the Allies, the Polish II Corps was destined to be a part of one of the most decisive battles of World War II.

Rome has been the capital of Italy for over 2,500 years. It is known as "The Eternal City." Rome has been considered the seat of the Papacy (Pope) since the 1st century A.D. (abbreviation for the Latin Anno Domini, which translates to "the Year of our Lord").

Adolf Hitler was a great admirer of imperial Rome and its form of government called an autocracy. B. C. stands for "Before Christ." Autocracy is a form of government where power is concentrated in the hands of one person.

Hitler believed that some ancient Germans had become part of the imperial Roman social fabric and exerted great influence on it. He even emulated the architecture of ancient Rome. Many of the edifices Hitler built were inspired by neoclassic Roman architecture. An edifice is a building, especially one of large size or imposing appearance. Zeppelinfeld Stadium in Nuremberg, Germany, where Nazi rallies were held each year, is an example of Hitler's neoclassical Roman architecture.

The terrain and cold winters of Italy made travel difficult. The snow was sometimes several feet deep. The soldiers traveled over narrow roads which were clinging to the sides of mountains and overlooking rivers and valleys a thousand feet below.

Wojtek was an active part of the unit all along the way. When the soldiers moved from one part of the country to the next, he could be found in the lead truck sitting in the passenger seat, as always, taking in all the beautiful surroundings of a country that had a 3,000-year history. On occasion astonished British troops would do a double take as the Polish II Corps would pass, and Wojtek would give them his best military salute.

Italy was part of the Axis Powers, as my dear readers probably remember. Rome is in the central region of Italy. Hitler used the natural defensive geography of central Italy, with its tall mountains and narrow passageways, to his great advantage. This beautiful but restrictive terrain (a tract of land with reference to its natural features and military advantages) made travel difficult at best. For centuries the capture of Rome had been a daunting and challenging affair even by history's most skilled armies.

Italy was unlike anything Wojtek had ever witnessed. Fog was a constant part of life. It drifted across the russet face of the mountains which were in deep contrast to the evergreen forest that consumed every inch of free soil below. Heavy, slate-colored clouds hung low over the landscape, trailing in gray wreaths down the sides of the fantastic hills. In the evening while the soldiers were making camp, Wojtek would sit and watch as the sun sank low, turning the sky to the west blazing shades of scarlet and gold. This beautiful kaleidoscope of colors seemed to bring back distant memories of a time when he played beneath his mother's feet as she traveled through the forest in Iran.

After weeks of brutal travel, the soldiers entered the town of Cassion. Cassion is located in a valley with rivers passing on its east and west sides. It is 130 kilometers (81 miles) from Rome. High atop the mountain which looks down on Cassion lies a historic hilltop abbey that was founded in A. D. 529 by a monk known as Benedict of Nursia. An abbey is a community devoted to religious life under a superior called an abbess. It was a huge castle made up of many buildings and consumed the entire top of the mountain. The abbey was called Monte Cassion. Monte in Italian means mountain.

ONCE A HERO

When the Benedictine monk selected this hill, he did so with great care. He saw that it provided an advantageous viewpoint from which to see far below in all directions. It was considered by the Romans, who lived in times past, as well as great military minds since, to be the best defensive and offensive vantage point in Italy. For over 1,484 years, this abbey had been sciential (having knowledge) of all who passed this way to Roma (Rome in English).

The Abbey of Monte Cassion was built over fourteen centuries (1,400 years) ago, but the town of Cassion is even older. Cassion was established twenty-four centuries (2,400 years) ago. The Roman general Marcus Antonius (Marc Antony in English) had a villa in Cassion. The Roman Legion marched this route to and from military campaigns from 30 B.C. to A. D. 284.

For centuries the abbey, which sat 1,700 feet above the valley floor, had been known as "The Gateway to Rome." With the advantage of height above the rugged terrain below, a small contingent of military troops in the abbey could hold at bay an entire battalion of well-armed and well-trained soldiers. The battle that was brewing between the Germans and the Allies would be known as the Battle of Monte Cassion. It would prove to be one of the bloodiest battles of World War II.

Several weeks before the Allied troops arrived in Cassion, German paratroopers parachuted into the Monte Cassion Abbey. The Germans were deeply entrenched in the hilltop monastery. Three previous Allied assaults on Monte Cassion had resulted in thousands of dead Allied soldiers. Over 16,000 American mountain infantry soldiers were killed in one month.

The Polish II Corps were called in to make an all-out final assault to capture the fortress. This would be the Polish II Corps' finest hour. Let us not forget, my dear readers, a soldier named Private Wojtek who was a member of this Polish unit. His contributions would not soon be forgotten.

CHAPTER XI

The One Who Has Power over Animals

Wojtek had gained a certain amount of notoriety among the Allied troops. Troops from nearby camps heard about this friendly beast by word of mouth and would pay him a visit from time to time. Wojtek sat on a metal munitions box in the evening around the camp. He could usually be found in an upright, sitting position, arms akimbo (crossed), graciously accepting treats in exchange for granting the curious an audience. Wojtek always appeared relaxed and genial (pleasantly cheerful). Inside that huge body was a huge heart. Wojtek was happy no matter the conditions as long as he was with his Polish comrades. His florid (showy) personality made him an instant hit with everyone that he met.

On one occasion, a small group of soldiers from India was camped near our Polish troops. The night was clear with millions of stars shining above the sky like a canopy. There was no fog, and the night was lit by the moon. Soldiers from various camps moved about enjoying the brief freedom from war.

An Indian soldier approached the Polish soldiers' camp and viewed Wojtek with curiosity. The Indian was tall with a dark complexion. His dark eyes had an almost hypnotic quality. There was an air of pertinacity (determination) about him. The soldier was dressed in military fatigues (military issue shirt and pants) with a heavy coat and a pagri sometimes called a dastar upon his head. A pagri or dastar is four to six yards of material that is wrapped around the head. It is also called a turban. He was among a group of Indian soldiers that had joined the

British Army. In his hand he held a large piece of chocolate. Solicitously (anxious or concerned) he approached Wojtek.

When the soldier got within a meter (three feet) of Wojtek, he stopped. He and Wojtek exchanged looks. The calmness of the gentle giant seemed to change the mood of the Indian soldier. His feeling of being anxious had been replaced with bellicosity (eagerness to fight) in his attitude. Turning his head from side to side in an attempt to ascertain his motives, Wojtek looked at the turban-headed soldier one eye at a time.

The soldier had a smirk on his face and held out the chocolate, clearly offering it to Wojtek. Wojtek being accustomed to generous offers of treats reached out to receive his gift, but as Wojtek attempted to accept the chocolate, the Indian soldier quickly withdrew it.

Wojtek was taken aback. The soldier then proceeded to break out into laughter that overtook his entire body. This was so funny to our Indian friend that he held his stomach he laughed so hard. Wojtek was dismayed and looked around to see if any of his comrades had seen what had just happened. He made low grunting noises as if trying to think this thing through.

Peter, Fabian, Henryk and Dominik were watching. They exchanged looks among themselves. Each of them was dumbfounded at what they had just seen. Dominik asked the soldier, "Are you trying to upset my friend?" Without waiting for an answer, he continued, "If you are and you should succeed, I can assure you that you will not like it."

The Indian soldier said, "Do not worry. In my country I am known as 'the one who has the power over animals.' Watch and you shall see how I will have this beast follow me around like a well-trained dog in a matter of minutes. But first I must show him who is boss. You will be amazed by my powers." Dominik just shook his head at the utter absurdity of what he had just heard.

Soldiers from other camps were beginning to gather around to watch this strange show. Dominik said, "I suggest you not push it too far. Remember you are toying with a full-grown bear." The Indian barely gave Dominik's words a thought and instead responded, "Not to worry. No animal, regardless of strength or size, can resist my control."

The soldier then proceeded to reach over and tap Wojtek on the nose three times, saying in a loud, harsh voice, "No! You do not get the chocolate until I am ready to give it to you." The Indian then stood in front of Wojtek for a few seconds as a teacher would do to his student.

After a while he again held out the chocolate for Wojtek to take, but this time Wojtek was not amused and had no interest in the chocolate. The tap on the nose, which hurt because of the soldier's long fingernails, and the harsh way in which the soldier had spoken left our gentle friend confused.

All of a sudden, Wojtek stood straight up on his hind legs. He had figured out what the Indian soldier wanted. Now he understood. The soldier wanted to wrestle! Wojtek could not have been happier. I am sure my dear readers remember how the playful Wojtek loved to wrestle with his comrades in Africa.

Suddenly with the speed of a striking cobra, Wojtek leaped forward and decided to play his version of football, which means you are the football and Wojtek is team bear. Wojtek now had a huge arm around the paralyzed soldier's waist. He tucked him tightly under his arm and began to look around to see who else wanted to play.

The soldiers from the other camps had gathered around to watch this spectacle. They were totally taken aback by what had just happened. Wojtek, thinking the soldiers intended to join in the fun as his Polish comrades had done in the past, charged the crowd with his human football tucked tightly under his arm. Instead of these soldiers wishing to wrestle, they looked on in horror at this giant bear running toward them carrying a man under his arm. To them it looked like Wojtek had just gotten dinner and was looking for dessert. They ran away in every direction.

Wojtek did not understand. These were his pals, his friends that had given him treats and loved to be with him. He suddenly stopped in bewilderment. Why were they running? Didn't they want to wrestle?

The Indian soldier's complexion had gone from a dark liver brown color to the pure white color of snow. He still held the chocolate in his hand. The soldier's face was frozen and displayed an expression of disbelief. His mind had ceased to function the instant Wojtek had sprung upon him and placed him under his arm. It was as if a switch in his head had turned off his brain to keep it from exploding. His face recorded the last message his brain had received before total shutdown.

The soldier's body was stiff as a board. He was so rigid that any attempt to bend this poor fellow would have surely resulted in him breaking. The soldier's face was frozen with a look one would have after realizing too late there was no water at the bottom of the swimming pool. His eyes were opened wide and not blinking. To the casual observer, he could have easily been a piece of stone sculpture. The most curious thing was his mouth. It was opened wide as if he were about to make a loud scream, but a sound had never come forth. The Indian soldier was in a state of suspended animation.

Wojtek looked about and seeing no one wanted to play became bored with the game and dropped the soldier to the ground. He walked over and returned to his seat with arms akimbo.

After a minute or two, the color in the Indian soldier's face began to return. His breathing had resumed. The soldier raised his body to a position where he was now on his hands and knees. His head began to move from side to side. It was unknown to him neither where he was nor the day or year. He had just returned from the dead. Slowly and cautiously, he rose to a one knee position and then looked around. "The one who held command over animals" saw Peter, Aleksy, Fabian, Henryk and Dominik looking on with pathos (pity or compassion) on their faces. He looked around for Wojtek and saw him sitting on his metal box. *Somehow the giant beast has lost interest in eating me*, he thought to himself.

After getting to his feet and regaining a certain amount of composure, he walked over to our Polish friends and said bombastically (spitefully), "Here is the chocolate. Please give it to the beast. It is better that he has this to eat than me. But beware, if I could not put him under my control your lives are certainly doomed." After the soldier left the scene on spaghetti legs that did not appear to be able to hold the weight of his body, Dominik said, "Wojtek—one, 'the one who has control over animals'—zero."

CHAPTER XII

Valor in Combat

The next day the fourth campaign to take Monte Cassion began. Wojtek had never been this close to the fighting. His comrades were concerned how he would react. Surprisingly instead of being afraid when the artillery shells began to explode and the staccato (short and rapid) sound of machine gun fire filled the air, Wojtek would climb to the tops of trees to get a better look at the action. This was no ordinary bear.

The soldiers were busy schlepping (carrying) artillery shells from the munitions trucks to the huge artillery guns up the hill. It was brutal, demanding, physical work. One day as Wojtek was watching the soldiers drooping from fatigue, making their trip up and down to the big guns, our giant beast decided he would help out. Wojtek ambled over to a truck, stood up on his hind legs, and gestured with his arms to one of the soldiers on the truck, signaling him to hand him one of the boxes.

The boxes contained artillery shells and had rope handles on each end for carrying purposes. It took two soldiers to carry each box of artillery shells. The boxes were heavy, weighing over 46 kilos (100 pounds) each. Soldiers positioned in the truck would each take the end of a box and hand it off to two other soldiers on the ground who would then proceed to carry the box of shells to the big guns.

The soldier that Wojtek gestured to was Aleksy. Aleksy said to the soldier who was in the truck with him, "Help me give the next box to my mate here." At the time Aleksy had spoken, the British soldier had his back to Wojtek and did not see him walk up. Turning around and seeing Wojtek with his arms stretched out with six-inch claws just inches from his face, the soldier was so startled that he jumped back falling over Aleksy. While on the floor of the truck, he looked up at Aleksy and said, "Are you mad? This is live ammunition."

Aleksy said, "Well, thank God for that. I thought we were shooting blanks at the bloody Krauts in hopes we could scare them to death. Come on, man, get off your butt and grab that box."

With that exchange, the two soldiers lifted the box of ammunition and handed it to Wojtek. Wojtek placed the box under his arm, and walking on his hind legs, he proceeded to carry it to the big guns where the ammo boxes were being stacked. Wojtek stacked the box perfectly and went back for another.

Over the next four months, the Polish troops delivered more than 17,000 tons of ammunition to the front lines. Wojtek did the work of two men each and every day. He worked tirelessly, day and night, bringing ammunition and supplies to the soldiers. During this entire time, Wojtek was never known to have dropped a single box of ammunition. The relentless shelling by the Polish artillery allowed the Allied forces to break through the Nazi defenses and capture Monte Cassion.

Wojtek's bravery in the face of battle amazed all who witnessed the heroic deeds of this majestic warrior. Only those who have shared the crucible (severe test) of war can truly understand what this noble, Nazi-fighting beast had just contributed to winning the battle of Monte Cassion.

Wojtek was so inspiring to his fellow soldiers that they wanted to come up with some way of recognizing their hirsute (hairy) hero. They knew Wojtek would never get a medal or anything of the sort. To the army, this was war and there was no time for foolishness like giving bears medals. So the Polish soldiers decided to champion the recognition Wojtek deserved themselves. They came up with an idea that would give the most beloved member of the Polish II Corps everlasting fame.

To be a hero fighting for a just cause and to be recognized by your fellow countrymen has honor attached. To be a hero among your fellow soldiers also has valor (boldness in facing great danger) attached.

The 22nd Artillery Supply Company Polish II Corps adopted a new insignia (distinguishing mark). Their new insignia was a bear walking upright and carrying an artillery shell. The Polish soldiers had their new insignia stamped into badges that the men wore on their uniforms. They had the Wojtek logo painted on all their trucks and every piece of equipment. The soldiers in the Polish II Corps proudly wore the insignia of "Wojtek" (the smiling warrior in Polish) for the remainder of the war. Wojtek and his comrades would go on to fight the Germans across the Italian peninsula, breaking through the enemy lines and forcing the Germans out of Italy.

The war had come to an end. The trek of the Polish soldiers had been long and difficult. It had also consumed many years of their lives. They were anxious to go home to their families. An agreement had been made between the British and Stalin that put Poland under Communist control. This was disheartening to the Polish soldiers. The Polish soldiers did not like the prospect of living in a Soviet police state, but it was home and where they hoped to find their families.

Deployment of the troops began with a few of the soldiers being released from duty early. Soldiers who had been wounded but were well enough to travel were chosen first. They immediately made their way to Poland but did not receive the welcome you might have expected. The remaining Polish II soldiers stayed in Italy waiting for orders to return home. While they waited, there was much celebration. In the midst of their end of war rejoicing, terrible news reached them. They learned that upon their arrival in Poland, the Polish soldiers released from duty had all been shot or imprisoned by the Communist regime. How could this be? After spending the last four years in hard labor and battle, these valiant soldiers had returned home just to be murdered. The soldiers had nowhere to turn. Once again they thought of their comrade, Father Josef.

Peter wrote:

My dear friend and comrade,

As you are aware, the war has ended. Our Polish comrades fought in a gallant spirit sacrificing much with hopes of one day returning to their homeland. The few who have returned were either shot or put in prison by the Communists. We are now men without a country. I request that you do whatever you can to help us find a place where we can live and be reunited with our families. I pray this letter finds you safe with all the vitality you possessed when I last saw you.

Peter

Through the years, Father Josef had managed to stay in contact with Werner, his Bavarian brother in spirit. Werner and Eva had settled in Switzerland where they lived on a small dairy farm with their daughter Hiya. Bubi was attending the university in Zurich studying engineering. Hans, having graduated from the university a few years earlier with a degree in law, was now living in the capital city of Bern. Hans worked as a legal counsel for the Swiss Parliament.

In the letter Father Josef explained the plight (unfortunate condition) of the Polish soldiers. The Swiss Parliament had very good relations with the British Parliament. Father Josef had high hopes that Hans could be of help in persuading the British to allow the Polish soldiers to live somewhere in the United Kingdom.

Through the efforts of Hans and Father Josef, the Polish soldiers and Wojtek were sent to Winfield Aerodrome on Sunwick Farm near Hutton, Berwickshire, in Scotland.

CHAPTER XIII

Wojtek Meets the Schoolmaster

Scotland was first settled about 10,000 years ago. In 55 B.C. (55 years before the birth of Christ), Julius Caesar, a general in the Roman Empire, invaded the islands with two Roman legions (a legion is 5,000 soldiers) and 2,000 cavalrymen (horse-riding soldiers). Caesar claimed the land as part of the Roman province of Britannia. The indigenous (native) people called this place Caledonia.

Despite building a Roman army of five legions (25,000 soldiers), the Romans could never conquer the indigenous people of Britannia. After four centuries (400 years) of battle, the Romans decided to pull up stakes and leave the islands forever. When the Romans left Britannia, not one Roman soldier remained behind; they totally abandoned Britannia. It could be said that the Romans eviscerated (removed the contents) Rome from the islands to save the "pride" of the Roman Legion. Up until this time, the Romans had never completely withdrawn from any land they had invaded. The Romans were considered to have the most powerful military force on earth. It was unthinkable that they could not conquer what they considered to be primitive tribes scattered among the islands. However unthinkable it may have been, the Romans did leave Caledonia with their tail between their legs.

Let us now, my dear readers, catch up with Wojtek and our good friends, the Polish soldiers. We will find the lovable Wojtek doing what he does best—attracting attention and winning hearts.

The Polish soldiers were settling into their new home at Sunwick Farm located in the rural parish of Hutton near Scotland's border with England. The beautiful Scottish countryside was very much to the liking of Wojtek and his Polish comrades. The soldiers were billeted (lodged) in barracks that had beds, toilets, showers and wood-burning stoves for heat. Wojtek was allowed to roam the camp as he pleased. It wasn't long before rumors were circulating around the countryside about a giant bear living among the Polish soldiers.

The soldiers had been demobilized and were temporarily put on the king's payroll. With the rank of private in the Polish II Corps, Wojtek received 12.18 British pounds Sterling (20 US dollars) per month, cigarettes, and food rations. This equaled the same pay and rations as any private in the king's service. The soldiers took this money and set it aside every month. They knew a sad reality would one day pay a visit at their front door: That day would come when they had to leave their cherished friend.

Peter, Aleksy, Fabian, Dominik and Henryk had families they were longing to see. They wanted to start new lives. Having no idea what they were going to do about their loyal comrade and friend, the soldiers were in hopes that the money would help find Wojtek a home where he would be cared for and loved. However, for the time being, they were together with their soldier-bear. The thought of leaving Wojtek behind was intolerable, and the soldiers pushed it to the back of their minds. After many years of hardships, they had learned to deal with what was at hand and let the future take care of itself.

Now that the war had been won, there were few restrictions pertaining to civilians visiting military compounds in Scotland. Every day visitors would come by the camp in hopes of catching a glimpse of this friendly beast. The Scottish people knew of Wojtek's exploits and were eager to see this Nazi-fighting bear up close. Children brought him candy and were allowed to ride on his back. If Wojtek saw someone smoking, he would stand on his hind legs, walk over and stick out a huge paw to bum a cigarette. But, of course, the cigarette had to be lit before it was accepted.

On weekends the soldiers would go into town. Wojtek was always a member of the group no matter where our Polish friends ventured.

ONCE A HERO

When the hero of Monte Cassion came into town, the Scottish people always gave him a welcome befitting any visiting dignitary. Anytime Wojtek graced a pub with his presence, this fun-loving beast would receive the golden key of hospitality, which meant everything was on the house (free to Wojtek and, many times, his Polish comrades). A pub (short for public house) is a family-friendly gathering place that offers the emptor (customer) food, beer, darts and lots of lively conversation.

One of the soldiers' favorite pubs was known as *The Brown Bear*. This particular pub had been in business for over one hundred years. Wojtek had his own seat where, on occasion, he sat as the guest of honor. Oftentimes he preferred to stand at the bar with his comrades.

One midday morning while Wojtek was standing at the bar with his comrades, he met an interesting Scottish gentleman. I will take a moment, my dear readers, and tell you about this brief encounter.

It was a Saturday. Wojtek and his comrades, Peter, Aleksy, Fabian, Dominik and Henryk, moseyed (strolled) into town and soon found themselves standing at the bar of *The Brown Bear*. For a bear that weighed 43 stone (602 pounds), Wojtek was very light on his feet. Not a sound came from his footsteps as he casually approached the pub. Once inside the pub, Wojtek stood on his hind legs and snuggled up to the bar.

At the bar stood a distinguished gentleman who was heavy in thought while diligently nursing his fourth pint of beer. He was talking sotto voce (low, soft voice not to be overheard) and unaware of anyone around him. The man was dressed in a tweed jacket, white shirt and plaid tie. He sported a well-trimmed beard with graying ginger-colored hair cropped neatly above the ears. The man wore round glasses that were held in place by pieces of thin wire looped behind each ear. The gentleman that I have just described was the local schoolmaster. He was well-known among the townspeople but rarely seen in any pub. The schoolmaster's wife did not approve of pubs. Our gentleman's name was Angus Magee.

Angus was just getting over a long illness which had kept him bedridden for many weeks. Now that he felt well again, he decided he would make a rare trip to the pub for a few pints.

Angus paid little attention when Wojtek and his buddies walked up to the bar. He happened to be standing next to Wojtek and began speaking to him without turning his head. "So, my good man, why don't you and I have a little tête-à-tête (French for private conversation)? Do you believe, as I do, that going to the pub and having a few pints is good for a man's mental health?"

By this time Wojtek had received his free pint of beer and was busy consuming his bounty. Aleksy had given Wojtek a lit cigarette. Whenever Aleksy smoked, he always lit one for Wojtek.

Angus continued without turning his head or waiting for an answer, " 'We need to address the cultural side of drinking,' I says to the missus this morning. 'A man must expand his mind. There is nothing better than a couple pints to expand a man's mind, so he is capable of handling the complex problems of day-to-day life.' She then has the nerve to tell me, 'Go on with you, Angus. Get all the culture you want, but you do it at the pub where the devil lives. You won't be partaking of demon spirits in my house!' "

"So I says, 'Woman, what do you know about drinking? You spend all your time down at the church gossiping with them other women who know nothing about a man expanding his mind. The vicar (a person acting as priest of a parish) goes to the pubs two or three times a week himself! Now, there's a man who knows a bit about the bennies (benefits) of a pint or two.' "

"Then she says, 'Don't go telling me what I know; I know plenty! You don't have to be a cow to know a thing or two about milk now, do you? The vicar is only there to convert sinners. Don't you go beseeching (begging) for an excuse because of your wicked ways? You are only trying to involve a good man like the vicar in Satan's work when he is doing work for the church. I won't have it, Angus. I know the truth. One day you are going to be in that pub, and Satan himself will be standing right there next to you. You better hope the vicar is in that den of sinners to save you, or the devil will take you away right then and there. I will have no drinking under my roof, and don't you forget it!' "

"Funny she says that," Angus hiccupped as he continued, "I thought I lived there, too. So I picks meself up, and here I stand improving me mental health with blokes like you who understand me. No woman is going to tell Angus Magee when he can and cannot expand his mind."

After this elocution (a person's manner of speaking) of double talk, this inebriated (drunk) gentleman began to take another drink from his pint of beer. At the same time, he glanced out the corner of his eye at Wojtek. Suddenly he froze. Angus' mind required a second opinion as to what he thought he had just seen.

His raised hand, holding the pint of beer inches from his mouth, had stopped in midair. Angus focused his eyes straight forward for the first time. He was now looking in the mirror located at the back of the bar. There, standing beside him, was what appeared to be a giant bear with a beer in his hand and a lit cigarette in his mouth. The huge beast had a Cheshire cat smile on his face as if to say, "Hi, Angus. I am here to take you with me."

In the mirror, everyone standing at the bar looked like normal blokes except the one standing next to Angus. He was beginning to have grave concerns about his theory of how drinking was the pathway of improving one's mental health.

Angus closed his eyes tightly and slowly reopened them. The beer-drinking, cigarette-smoking bear with the Cheshire cat smile was still there standing next to him. His wife's words from that morning flashed through his brain, "*One day you are going to be in that pub, and Satan himself will be standing right there next to you.*"

Slowly Angus lowered his glass and placed it on the bar. The confusion enveloping the schoolmaster's state of mind was plainly written on his face. His brow went from having deep, wrinkled furrows to his forehead being stretched so tight that his spectacled eyes were as big as saucers. Without ever turning toward Wojtek, he moved in the opposite direction toward the door. Quickly he made his way out the door and vanished outside the pub.

His wife never knew why he returned home so suddenly that day. She had not been expecting him for several hours. The only thing she knew for certain was, from that day forward, he was a changed man. Angus attended church every Sunday and never touched another drop of demon spirits. He even joined the choir! Perhaps drinking does improve one's mental health. It certainly helped to expand the mind of Angus Magee.

CHAPTER XIV

Wojtek and the Sword Dance

After enjoying a few pints at *The Brown Bear*, Wojtek and his comrades decided to venture out into the streets of the town. They followed the sound of bagpipes that had just started playing. Bagpipes, that are akin to Scottish tradition, were actually introduced to Britannia by the Romans. Unbeknownst to our Polish friends, the local townsfolk had organized a dance contest. All the town lasses (ladies) were invited to compete to see who was the best Highland Fling dancer. The winner would be recognized as the best Highland Fling dancer in the parish. This was a great honor.

The streets were filled with people offering all types of baked goodies, cheese, beer and haggis. Good cheer filled the streets. There were dueling bagpipes in an alcove adjacent to the corner of town square. Dancing in the alcove in front of the bagpipes were three ginger-haired Scottish lasses. The Highland Fling contest was about to begin, but first, my dear readers, allow me to take a moment and answer the question you must have about haggis. I will also share with you the remarkable history of the Highland Fling.

Haggis is uniquely Scottish. It is a savory sort of pudding that contains a sheep's heart, liver and lungs. These are minced with onion, oatmeal, suet (hard white fat on the kidneys of sheep) and other spices. This combination of ingredients is mixed and encased in the sheep's stomach which is then cooked for three hours. Haggis has a long history and is a very popular dish in Scotland. Haggis is now a product that Scottish merchants export around the world.

In days past, the Highland Fling was known as the "Gillie Callum." It was also known as "The Scottish Sword Dance." The "Gillie Callum" or "Sword Dance" was only performed by men. The dance began with two swords being placed on the ground in an "X" shape. The dancer then danced around within the four quarters of the "X."

Tradition says the original Gillie Callum was a Celtic prince who lived in 1054. The dance is said to date back to King Malcolm Canmore (Shakespeare's MacBeth). Prince Callum is said to have crossed his own bloody claymore (a two-handed broadsword) over the bloodier sword of the defeated chief and danced over them both in exultation (triumphant joy).

At the turn of the century, World War I, referred to as the Great War, had taken most of the Scottish men into battle. The Sword Dance, which would become known as the "Highland Fling" because of its association with the people who lived in the Scottish Highlands, was becoming a thing of the past. There were very few men left in Scotland to keep the tradition alive. However, the Scottish women refused to give up their heritage. As a tribute to their husbands and sons who were fighting in battle, the women began to dance the Highland Fling. The women of Scotland saved this proud tradition, and today the Highland Fling is performed almost exclusively by women.

At the dance contest were three ginger-haired Scottish lasses who wore tartan (a woolen cloth woven in a distinctive plaid color) skirts and special shoes known as ghillies. It is a soft shoe similar to a ballet shoe. The girls had brightly colored knee socks, white shirts and black vests. Dancing with their toes pointed and their arms held high at different angles above their heads, the dancers sprang from one foot to the next in a graceful cadence that appeared to be free of gravity. The crowd was clapping in a rhythmic beat as these young lasses danced the Highland Fling. The music of the bagpipes was resounding (loud and strong) and spread across the town.

Wojtek and his comrades were enjoying the gaiety (cheerful spirits) of the music and the artistic movements of the dancers. The Polish soldiers started clapping along with the crowd. Wojtek started clapping along with the soldiers and then stood on his hind legs and began moving his head up and down to the rhythm of the music.

It was as if these colorful, athletic, dancing lasses with their graceful kicks and twirling bodies were inviting our magnanimous Warrior to join them. Wojtek could not resist such an invitation.

On his hind legs, Wojtek walked from the crowd to the center of the alcove where the Scottish lasses were dancing. Never having danced before did not stop our noble hero from performing the most erythematic (rhythmic with gaiety) Highland Fling that anyone had ever known a bear to perform. He held both arms above his head and shifted from one foot to the next in a capering (to leap or skip) movement. Wojtek kept perfect time with the music. The girls would twirl. Wojtek would twirl. They would jump and kick, and the Smiling Warrior would do the same.

The crowd could not believe their eyes. No one really believed all the stories they had heard about Wojtek. The Battle of Monte Cassion was a turning point of the war. This was true, but a bear could not really have been a part of this battle. Then again, no one could believe what they were actually seeing now—a giant, dancing bear doing the Highland Fling with the three pretty lasses. Perhaps the testimony of the soldiers was true.

While all this was going on, two young lads were providing the most fantastic bagpipe music since the time the Celtic prince led his troops into battle with bagpipers sounding the charge. It was a sound of celebration, glory and honor. It brought back a moment in time when the Scottish people of old had defeated the Roman legions many centuries before. Before long the entire crowd broke out into dance. The fun went on until the moon was high up in the star-studded sky and continued until it disappeared to a patient death and gave way to the birth of morning.

CHAPTER XV

Wojtek Finds a New Home

Time moved on, and the soldiers were getting anxious to move their lives forward. They had been in Sudwick Farms for a year. During his time in Scotland, Peter had greatly improved his ability to speak the English language and as a result had been able to acquire a job as a construction worker in London. He had already sent his wife in Poland money so she and the children could join him. Peter told his new employer that he would report for work in approximately one month.

Fabian and Henryk were on their way to Munich, Germany. They had secured jobs as apprentice clock makers. Aleksy was going to America. Detroit, Michigan, a town that would become known as the motor city, would be his new home. Plants that had been used to make machines for war were being retooled to make cars. Aleksy was getting in on the ground floor of the automotive, industrial phenomenon. The thought of going to America fueled his imagination with many possibilities.

The soldiers were on the threshold of a much-earned new beginning. There was only one problem waiting to be resolved: What to do about Wojtek? After many inquiries, Peter learned that Edinburg, Scotland, had a zoo complete with two veterinarians and a staff capable of taking care of a variety of animals. The zoo was located on 35 hectares (87 acres) on the outskirts of the capital of Scotland.

Peter wrote the Edinburg Zoo and asked if they could provide a loving home to a Syrian bear weighing 43 stone (603 pounds) and needing much affection. In his letter Peter stated how Wojtek had been a part of the soldiers' lives since he was only one stone (10 pounds) and explained all the adventures they had shared as Wojtek grew to be-

ONCE A HERO

come a full-grown bear. Wojtek, he continued, had even saved the soldiers' lives and served bravely beside them in battle. It was obvious by Peter's letter that emotions ran high at the thought of leaving Wojtek.

The soldiers were determined not to leave their beloved comrade without, somehow, someway, ensuring he would have food, comfortable shelter, and most of all, a loving family.

The Edinburg Zoo wrote back to Peter that indeed they could provide a home for Wojtek. The zoo officials knew the story of Wojtek. They had no doubt that people would come far and wide to meet this Nazi-fighting hero bear. Wojtek was a celebrity in Scotland and would be a huge draw to attract people to the zoo.

The Edinburg Zoo was excited about the fact that Wojtek would soon be making the zoo his home. They spread the news far and wide. The response was great among the Scottish population, and the European community as a whole. Unfortunately, it attracted the attention of a very devious man that would try to use Wojtek as a propaganda tool. This man, my dear readers, was Joseph Stalin.

Stalin and the Communist Party were firmly in control of Poland. Wojtek was a symbol of freedom and the power of the human spirit which can win against all odds. He represented everything the Communist Party was not. With the Communist Party in control, Poland was a police state. Everything was controlled by the state, and the people were ruled by the iron fist of Stalin.

Stalin maintained that Wojtek was a soldier in the Polish army, and as such, he was a citizen of Poland and should be returned to Poland. He went on to say they had made a home for the hero of Monte Cassion in the Warsaw Zoo. Warsaw is the capital of Poland. Stalin insisted that he only wanted to ensure that Wojtek would be safe and well cared for.

When the Polish soldiers heard of Stalin's demand for Wojtek, they were furious. Stalin's insouciance (lack of care or concern) for the Polish people was very well-known by the soldiers. They could only imagine the conditions to which Wojtek would be subjected. How could anyone believe Stalin had any concern for Wojtek's safety? Stalin was well-known to prevaricate (speak falsely or mislead) whenever it would serve his purpose.

The soldiers contacted the Edinburg Zoo officials and beseeched them to not let Stalin get his hands on Wojtek. The zoo officials said it was out of their control. Their instructions not to interfere came from the highest levels of the British government.

The British government was inclined to give in to Stalin's demands rather than risk damaging diplomatic relations with the newly-installed Communist Party in Poland. The British were still badly crippled because of the huge losses they had incurred during the war. At the same time, they did not want to anger the Scottish people. The British knew Wojtek was a very popular celebrity in Scotland. To save face on both fronts, they decided to conduct furtive (secretive) communication with Stalin. The Brits were hopeful the matter could be handled quietly without it becoming a tumultuous (violent) affair in Scotland.

My dear readers, over the past five years, the soldiers had encountered many hardships. In the beginning, they were strong and courageous individual men who began working together just to survive, each having his own special skill. The myriad of impossible obstacles they were forced to overcome had changed that equation. Now, they were forged into a single, united strength with undefeatable determination and force. The soldiers heard of the furtive talks between the Brits and Stalin and were determined not to surrender their comrade to Stalin.

The soldiers circulated a request to have a town meeting. This was on a Monday. The town's mayor, Patrick Fitzpatrick, known as Paddy, called for a meeting to be held in town square the following Saturday. On the day of the meeting, the square was filled with every man, woman and child of the parish. The people of the parish had heard of

Stalin's demand to have Wojtek sent to the Warsaw Zoo in Poland. Wojtek had become a much-admired and loved member of the Scottish community. The people, not only in this parish but also in all of Scotland, threw themselves into the battle to save Wojtek from the hubris (arrogance) of Stalin. The soldiers and the town council had devised a solution to the dilemma.

The mayor announced that there was going to be a special election. The election was being held to fill a newly-created position on the town council. He went on to say there would be only one candidate that had qualified to run for this position. His name was Wojtek Bear, formerly a private in the Polish army. The vote would be taken this day in the afternoon, and the successful candidate would be installed in this new position immediately following the election. The crowd was ecstatic. The shouting and cheering for council candidate Wojtek Bear was so resounding that it awoke Stalin from a dead sleep in Moscow.

Wojtek Bear was elected by a landslide that day and became a citizen of Scotland. Stalin had no claim to a citizen of Scotland. The soldiers and the people of Scotland had saved the Smiling Warrior from a most certain drastic fate.

On November 15, 1947, a pickup truck arrived at Winfield where Wojtek and the soldiers were billeted. Wojtek climbed into its bed and was driven to his new home at the Edinburg Zoo. Aleksy, Fabian, Dominik, Henryk and Peter were on hand to bid their beloved comrade farewell. Peter accompanied Wojtek on the trip. Once at the zoo, Wojtek was taken to the enclosure where he would stay. He and Peter entered the enclosure together. Peter stayed for a while then hugged his friend, said goodbye and left.

Peter moved to London and began his new job as a construction worker. He was later reunited with his wife and children. Of all Wojtek's close friends, Peter was the only one who never returned to see him again. He had lived through so many traumas over the past five years, being with his wife and children was a dream come true.

Wojtek had been by his side the entire time. When asked why he never returned to see his friend again he said, "Leaving Wojtek nearly broke me. The thought of going back was too painful."

Many of the soldiers resettled in the U.K. (United Kingdom) and traveled to see their friend often. The zookeepers pretended not to notice when Wojtek's war comrades climbed into the enclosure to share a beer and smoke. Sometimes to the amazement of the zoo's visitors, they would wrestle with their friend for old-time sake. When they would leave, Wojtek slipped into a funk that lasted for days. He could not understand why his friends left, and he could not go with them.

Over time Wojtek began to bond with the public that came to see him. When he heard someone speaking Polish, he would stand on his hind legs and wave to the crowd. Young children who were born to the Polish soldiers would often come by and sing the Polish national anthem. Wojtek would always respond by waving and dancing which always brought squeals of joy from the children and smiles to their faces.

As the years passed, the stories of Wojtek began to fade away. Even the plaque honoring this Nazi-fighting bear at the Edinburg Zoo was taken down. He was a popular attraction at the zoo until his death in December 1963. Wojtek passed away at the age of 22.

Since his death, Wojtek, the hero of Monte Cassion and the most famous soldier of the Polish II Corps, has gained a renewed interest. In Poland, Edinburgh, the Imperial War Museum in London, and the Canadian War Museum, there are statues of him and plaques memorializing the lives he saved.

In 2009 the Scottish Parliament made plans to erect a statue of Wojtek and Peter, who died in 1968, standing side by side. These two proud warriors have since been reunited.

You have now been told the true story, my dear readers, of the bear who helped to win a war. Let us never forget this brave hero and what he represents—courage in the face of adversity. Wojtek, the

ONCE A HERO

Smiling Warrior, will live forever in the hearts of those who are willing to sacrifice all for the sake of freedom. Carry on, our gallant Warrior, carry on.

THE END

CPSIA information can be obtained at www.ICGtesting.com
Printed in the USA
LVOW11s0705301115

464646LV00001B/51/P